DEATH AND DIVINATION

DEBRA DUNBAR

debra dunbar
FIENDISHLY FUN FICTION

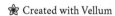

CHAPTER 1

NASH

I died a little that first time I saw her. And each time after that, I died a little more.

Mortal lives are brief as a spark and a reaper's only interaction with them is when that spark flickers and dies. We are there at the very end, watching and waiting. And when the fire had gone out and all that remains is a rapidly cooling ember, we go to work. We are viewed as the harbingers of death, but increasingly the mortals are able to snatch a soul back just before we sever it. Sometimes a miracle happens and what should have been an extinguished flame springs to life again.

A miracle.

In my case, it wasn't a miracle; it was a reaper not doing his job. That soul should have been freed from his mortal form, but I delayed, entranced by the woman who was bent over him, fighting to keep him alive. That delay meant the man lived. It was a technicality, but I felt the effects shiver through me, changing me forever. It was then I knew that one day I'd be faced with a choice—and *that* would not be a mere technicality. Allowing a mortal to escape the embrace

1

of death was a dereliction of duty. The born must die. It's not a reaper's place to delay or circumvent that cycle. We are not here to grant life or death. We are not here to decide. We are only here to assist death in taking its course.

I know. I'm a real downer at parties. But then, no one actually *invites* a reaper to a party. When one of us shows up uninvited, that usually spells the end of the party right then and there. Maybe if we occasionally got invited to a party, we'd be less morose.

I've attended a few parties—uninvited of course. They do seem as if they'd be quite enjoyable under normal circumstances. Sadly, by the time I arrive, it's usually because someone has gotten drunk and fallen off a balcony or passed out in the hot tub while his friends weren't looking, or decided driving the four-wheeler off the garage roof was a good idea.

Observe. Wait. Reap the soul. It's a pretty straightforward sort of job. Except for the one time everything changed—that one time I waited too long.

There she was. And the second I saw her, I was transfixed.

"Live. Please, live," she'd muttered as she leaned over a man still seated in a wrecked car. Snaking a tube down the man's throat, she attached a bag. A co-worker squeezed the bag and she moved to cut the man's shirt sleeve off to attach an IV.

The vehicle looked as if the doors and roof had been pried open. Broken glass and bits of metal scattered nearby along with what seemed to be the contents of several grocery bags. I'd seen this sort of thing a million times, but I'd never seen *her* before. I could feel the victim's soul began to separate from his body, but all I could do was watch this woman as she worked.

"How far out is transport?" she asked.

"Less than two. They're coming over the mountain now,"

a woman behind her replied.

"The spreader's in place to crack the floor," a man told her.

She nodded. "Tell transport we've got a hot load. Flora, have a splint ready to stabilize his leg. Ricky, get another IV bag ready to go."

I saw the curl of magic around her hands. The sight of it broke me from my trance and I moved closer. Her magic wasn't of a healing nature as I'd assumed it would be. No, it was a much more powerful talent. The woman who had so mesmerized me that I'd forgotten my task was a witch, and the magic that surrounded her in a kaleidoscope of color was divination.

She was an *oracle*.

I caught my breath and took a step back in respect. A healer witch...well, those mortals we generally rolled our eyes at, acknowledging that a powerful healing witch had the ability to stop us in our tracks. But it was only a delay. In the end, we always reaped our soul. No healing magic in the world could do more than extend a mortal life just a moment in the scheme of things.

But divination.... No reaper could see the future. To not only perceive the complex web that makes up the multi-dimension of time, but to *understand* it? To know which threads to follow? To know the outcome, even if that outcome is crouched in probabilities?

That was talent—a gift that the very universe bowed down to.

But even an oracle couldn't influence the future, only give it voice. Death was inevitable. Surely the beautiful woman with the hair as dark as the underworld itself could see that in her magic.

The sound of helicopter blades filled the air. "Transport's landing," a woman toward the back of the scene announced.

The witch set her jaw. "On three, Skip. One. Two. Three."

Skip engaged a hydraulic device and the floor of the mangled vehicle came apart. The three quickly pulled the victim from the car, stabilizing his leg with a splint and rolled blankets.

"Pulse is one-forty," Ricky called out as he replaced the bag of fluids.

"Transport has landed. They're ready and saying they could use help," the woman behind them shouted.

"I'll go," the witch said. "You all head back once we're airborne."

With a synchronized movement they'd clearly done thousands of times before, the three lifted the stretcher, moving the victim carefully toward the helicopter, and ducking low under the blades. Then they slid the victim in through the open door of the helicopter. The witch hopped in beside them and without hesitation, so did I. With a slam, the door closed, and the helicopter swayed as it took to the air.

"Pulse is dropping," one of the other paramedics said.

"Come on. Come on!" The witch pleaded as she checked a monitor. Her lips trembled, eyes shining with unshed tears. "Come on!" The magic swirling around the witch widened. Brightened. "He'll make it. He's going to make it."

I tilted my head and regarded her with a puzzled frown. No. I was here to collect a soul—this soul. He *wasn't* going to make it. Edging closer, I saw that the witch's lips were tight, trembling. I saw the shadows under her high cheekbones, saw the long thin fingers that pressed the bag with sure rhythm. Then, suddenly, she looked up and her eyes met mine.

Shocking blue eyes. In a pale face that looked as if it were chiseled from marble, her eyes were a clear cerulean blue. I felt something inside me stir, come to life. And in response, I felt something die.

"He'll make it," the woman said as if she were speaking directly to me. Magic snapped and crackled like electricity. "He'll make it."

Could she see me? How could she see me? Not that it mattered. All that mattered was the blue of her eyes, the full softness of her lips, the icy perfection of her skin, the inky darkness of her hair. Looking at her, I felt as if I were seeing the completed circle, the cold darkness of death and the bright brutal spark of color that was life.

It sounds so cliché, but I shook in my boots. Gripping my scythe, I fought the urge to reach out and touch her.

"Pulse is stable!" the other mortal announced. The man on the stretcher, the man who was supposed to be dead, stirred.

Crap. How embarrassing. He should have died when we were down on the ground. He should have died five minutes ago. He should have died, but I'd been too busy gawking at this beautiful witch, and now it was too late.

Too late for me, anyway.

The witch checked the IV bag, then looked directly into my eyes. "Who are you?" she demanded. "*What* are you?"

She could *see* me. What should have been a disconcerting realization instead made me unreasonably happy.

"Who are you talking to?" the other mortal asked.

She ignored him. "What are you?" This time she reached out and placed a hand on my chest. It felt as if the heat of her burned right through my robes to a physical form I was not supposed to have.

"I'm Death," I told her, reluctantly easing away from the warmth of her hand.

Then I left, failing to reap the soul I'd been sent to collect, praying to the unknown force that gave me purpose that I would have the occasion to see her again.

CHAPTER 2

TWO YEARS LATER - OPHELIA

"Cassie!" I shouted, walking into my sister's house.

Home. This place would always be home to me. I remembered my grandmother, the witch who'd run things in Accident until her death. I remembered my mother, the woman who'd left when I was nine for parts unknown. What I remembered the most, though, was Cassie. When mom took off after Grandma's death, Cassie at thirteen had muscled her way to the front, protecting and caring for the six of us girls until we were grown and on our own. She'd been an immovable power, an irresistible force, using her witch magic to convince a judge to emancipate her at thirteen and to grant her guardianship over six younger sisters.

She was the most powerful witch I'd ever known—and that included my grandmother. I admired her more than I ever wanted to admit. I downright worshipped her. If only I had half of her skill...

But I didn't. Where Cassie could perform a wide range of magic and cast a spell on the fly, I was specialized. Divination. And my divination most of the time was about as useful as a freezer at the North Pole. Sometimes the future was a sharp clear line. Sometimes it was an incomprehensible blur. Sometimes I interpreted that blur in a way that was absolutely wrong. It made me feel like a fool, like an inept amateur. It made me almost want to quit doing magic sometimes.

As if. Magic was like the breath in my lungs. An accurate divination usually required a ritual and certain focus objects and chants, but sometimes it happened like a flash without any effort at all. I could no sooner give it up than give up breathing.

"Cassie!" I shouted, making my way to the kitchen. It had become important to loudly announce your arrival at my family home. Now that my sister's demon mate had moved in...well, none of us wanted to walk in on the two of them doing it up against the kitchen counters.

Well, no one except my twin sister Sylvie, who would probably critique their performance and give them pointers and some accessories, all to keep their relationship sexually healthy.

How could identical twin sisters be so different? We both looked the same but around age five, we'd each gone in opposite directions, proving that identical DNA didn't necessarily mean identical people.

"Here! In the attic!" Cassie's voice filtered down from the top reaches of the house.

I climbed the stairs heading to the back room were the attic ladder was located. The house had been originally built a few hundred years ago, a one room house with a loft. Over the centuries, various additions had meant bedrooms, a kitchen, indoor plumbing, and an attic which housed furniture that was too dated to live downstairs but too sentimental to take to the dump, as well as boxes of belongings from our ancestors.

And the diaries. And the spell books.

Our witch ancestor, Temperance Perkins, had escaped the burning times and headed south and west, establishing our town as a haven for those of her kind. It had quickly become a haven for the supernatural, with Perkins witches as the caretakers throughout the centuries. Recently, Cassie had finally taken her place as head witch of the town.

And me? My job was to support her any way she needed. Well, that and my non-witch job as a paramedic for the Accident Fire Department. Most of our calls were for issues related to the supernatural residents, but we also served sections of the county that lay outside of our town's wards, so I found myself providing emergency medical attention to not only mermaids, fairies, werewolves, and trolls, but humans who were within our areas of service.

Which was what had happened tonight. Just thinking about that wreck tonight set my hair on end.

That woman had almost died. In fact, for a moment there, it had been touch and go. I was surprised she'd lived. What I hadn't been surprised about was the presence of the man who seemed to be at every serious call I'd been on. The man who I'd begun to think put his finger on the scale and occasionally allowed someone to live when they probably shouldn't have.

Don't get me wrong—there were still those who died either before I got there, during our assistance, or later at the hospital. But too many times when someone's life hung precariously in the balance, I got the impression fate, or something else, was giving things a little nudge in my favor.

I found Cassie on the attic floor, surrounded by books and what looked to be a cheese and summer sausage platter. No doubt her demon, Lucien, had brought it up to her. He was trying to do that delicate dance of giving Cassie her space and being caring. Personally, I think he could be glued to her side twenty-four-seven and she'd be thrilled. She'd complain, but she'd be thrilled. Her previous relationship had been with a panther shifter who'd cheated on her left and right, all while proclaiming devoted love. I was pretty sure Marcus had meant the devoted love thing, but a panther shifter had a different idea of fidelity than a human witch. There was no doubt in anyone's mind that Cassie's demon was physically and emotionally faithful. It warmed my heart to see them together. Lucien's attentiveness gave Cassie a pampered feeling she hadn't had since my grandmother had died.

"How are things going?" I asked.

Cassie rolled her eyes. "Oh, the usual. The gnomes tunneled through the west end, stole Emma's lawn flamingos, and refused to give them back. Instead of going to the sheriff, Emma went over and burned down their vegetable garden. The *gnomes* had enough sense to go to the sheriff, and when he found out it was Emma, he came to me."

I grimaced. Sheriff Oakes was a dryad and was perfectly capable of handling conflict and crime among most of our supernatural community. Most of them. Emma, however, was a chimera with an incredible sense of self-worth. In her eyes, there was a strict hierarchy of beings in the town of Accident, and a dryad was pretty far down on her registry of who's who. She hadn't considered witches to be much higher than dryads until an incident a few weeks ago when Cassie had magically levitated her and refused to let her down until she apologized to Fernando for calling him a rot-scaled gecko with creosote breath.

Fernando was a dragon. Dragons take insults very seriously. And nobody wants a pouty, offended dragon in their town.

Emma had floated in the air for a few hours before she finally gave in and offered Fernando a grudging apology which he accepted with surprising speed. Cassie had been amazed.

I hadn't been amazed. The pair would be doing it by next Tuesday, married by October, and hatching a little chimera-dragon baby before the buds bloomed on the cherry trees next year. And I was keeping totally mum about that vision because that was one future I didn't want to mess up.

A little chimera-dragon. Ooh, I couldn't wait for the baby shower. Hopefully Emma would let me babysit occasionally, although if Fernando treated his kid at all like he treated his treasure, no one in town would get within a hundred feet of the baby until it was legally able to vote.

"So, does Emma have her lawn flamingos back?" I asked.

Cassie nodded. "And the gnomes have to come by each night for the next month to bestow luck on her yard. Emma has to replant the burned garden at her cost, down to every last veggie plant."

"She doesn't have hands," I pointed out, wondering how the chimera was going to replant a garden with goat feet. Or a lion head. Or a serpent tail.

My sister shrugged. "Not my problem. She can dig, put the plant in with her mouth, then tamp it down with those cloven hooves. She's gotta learn that if you're going to burn something, you're gonna have to pay for it."

"Oh, really?" I grinned, remembering Cassie setting her ex-boyfriend's pants on fire in the middle of the courthouse.

"I paid for that. I'm still paying for that. I've got to attend anger management meetings every Friday night until I'm dead and in the grave," she shot back.

"Good thing you're going to end up immortal," I teased. "I wonder if they have anger management meetings in hell, where you'll be a princess or something. Perks of bonding with the son of Satan, right?"

"Oh, there are plenty of perks beyond that." She wiggled

her eyebrows and I immediately thought of the two of them naked and sweaty in bed. Lucky duck. Lucien was totally hot. Not my type at all, but totally hot. And yes, I was just a little bit jealous over my sister's fortune in the love department.

Maybe someday I'd be as lucky.

"How are things with the werewolves?" I asked, half afraid of what she might say.

"Dallas has made a move to break up Clinton's faction and reclaim that section of the mountain. He's made some headway, and I fully expect Clinton to retaliate next week some time."

I thought of the visions I'd been having the past two weeks and winced. "Do you think it will come to war? Bloodshed? Death?"

"I don't know. The last alpha war was bloody and brutal. A lot of wolves died or were executed after it was all over. But this is different. Clinton is Dallas' son, and I think they're both reluctant to take that step. I don't think either one really wants to kill the other, but I fear if there's no resolution to this, that's where we're headed."

"Can you just forbid it?" I was half pleading with her, sick at the thought of what sort of slaughter a war among the werewolves might bring. I wasn't a huge fan of the pack. I'd always considered the werewolves to be a bunch of backward bullies. But I didn't want them dead. I didn't want *anyone* dead.

"Sure, then I'd have a different war on my hands. Both factions would unite and try to wipe us out instead." Cassie ran a hand through her dark hair. "I'm trying to be diplomatic here—and yes, I know how amusing that sounds. Me. Diplomatic. But the werewolves have been allowed to have their own rules and their own culture for nearly two hundred years. I can't just walk in and smash that. I've insisted they bring their pack law into alignment with

11

certain fundamental town laws, and I've instituted a sanctuary policy for any wolf that wants to leave the pack. Those two things have pissed Dallas and Clinton off enough. I don't want to push it too far too fast."

"I don't want anyone to die." I sucked in a ragged breath and slowly let it out, trying to keep the panic at bay. Every time I faced death, whether in my paramedic job or in a divination, I saw myself as some sort of crusader, fighting to hold back fate, to allow someone just a while longer in this world. In reality, I knew how powerless I was. Perhaps the people I saved weren't meant to die. Perhaps those whose deaths I'd averted hadn't been predestined to lose their life that day after all. Maybe it was all an illusion and I was tilting at windmills, believing I was making a difference, all while the grim reaper mocked me and took whom he pleased.

Grim reaper. The man at my emergency calls. Was he really Death as he'd said, or a ghost, or something else entirely? When I'd first seen him, he'd been a figure in robes, a man with black lifeless eyes in an indistinct face. But over the last two years he'd changed. Morphed. Become someone who made my heart speed up in a good way when I saw him. Become someone I'd considered to be... well, hot.

How sick was that?

"What's wrong?" Cassie's forehead creased with concern and she reached over to place a hand on my cheek, just as she used to do when we were children. "You look tired, Ophelia —tired and...defeated."

I didn't want to tell her what was wrong. I didn't want to tell her about my strange fantasies of battling death. And I *didn't* want to tell her about the disturbing visions I'd been having. They were too confusing, too vague. I didn't want to worry her about something that we had no way of combating—at least not until I figured out exactly what it was we needed to deal with.

"It was a rough night at work last night," I said instead. "A pixie overdosed on persimmon seeds, there was a merman with a torn fin who nearly bled out, and Silas Crabtree got his tail caught in the sliding door at the twenty-four-hour grocery."

"Again?" Cassie rolled her eyes.

"Again. That wasn't the worst, though. There was a wreck out on the interstate. Six cars, one of them with an ejection. It was touch and go for a moment. We weren't sure if she was going to pull through."

"But she made it?" Cassie's eyes searched mine. She knew how upset I got in the face of death. As I child I'd sobbed over smushed earthworms and every roadkill. My youngest sister, Babylon, had taken to re-animating any animal body we came across in an effort to console me. It hadn't worked but try telling a five-year-old that the zombie frog hopping around the pond wasn't the same as the pre-death version.

I know. Paramedic probably wasn't the best choice of careers for someone who was gutted every time a patient didn't make it, but it felt like a calling. I felt as if somehow, I could singlehandedly hold back death. If I could save just one person through my efforts, then it was worth the personal anguish I went through each day.

"Yes, she made it. If she hadn't been a gargoyle, it would have been a different story." I cleared off a space and sat down next to my eldest sister, thinking there was one thing I *could* confide. "I've got a weird question, though. What do you know about ghosts?"

"Uh, nothing. The closest any of us is to a spirit worker is Babylon."

I shuddered. "Necromancy doesn't have anything to do with ghosts or spirits. It's animating the dead."

"Sometimes it does," Cassie argued. "A skilled necro-

13

mancer can hold a spirit in check, straddling both worlds. A bit in their body, a bit in the afterlife."

That whole thing gave me the heebie-jeebies. I loved my youngest sister, but her skill creeped me out. "I really hope Lonnie isn't doing that. It's bad enough when she does the reanimated corpse thing. Do you remember Thanksgiving?"

"How could I forget?" Cassie drawled.

Babylon had drunk too much wine and animated the turkey. Suffice it to say we ended up having take-out Chinese for Thanksgiving dinner.

"Well, I think I've been seeing a ghost," I told my sister. "For years now, I've been seeing someone at my calls. He's always at the ones where there's a critical or serious injury. It happened again last night. I was working on the gargoyle, and suddenly the guy was there. He was standing near us, looking at me. He does that. Usually when we go to load the person in the bus, and I look for him again he's gone."

"A bystander?" Cassie suggested.

"The police were keeping everyone back. It was a terrible accident—no one needed to be gawking at that. Besides, he was inside the police line."

"Maybe he managed to get past the police? Maybe it was a relative of the injured gargoyle, or another first responder?"

"At every serious call in the last two years?" I shook my head. "He's definitely not a first responder. And no one would have allowed a relative that close while we were working on someone. And if they had, why would a family member suddenly vanish?"

"He ran off to puke because the sight of blood freaked him out?" Cassie shrugged. "I doubt it was a ghost, Ophelia. You were focused, running on adrenaline, and trying to keep that gargoyle alive. Maybe you imagined it, or maybe it *was* a friend or family member and you just didn't notice him afterward."

"The same friend of different victims for two years?"

"You were probably mistaken. Those humans, they all look alike," she joked.

"You don't believe in ghosts," I accused her. "Seriously. You're a witch with six witch sisters, all of us performing magic and living in a town with goblins, and vampires, and werewolves, and mermaids but you don't believe in ghosts? You're knocking boots with a demon, but you don't believe in ghosts?"

She threw up her hands. "I'm sorry, I *don't* believe in ghosts. I've seen all of us do magic. I've seen goblins, vampires, werewolves, mermaids and more. I've seen what Lucien can do. I've never seen a ghost."

Death. He'd said he was Death, but I refused to believe that. Death freaked me out enough without the thought of one of death's minions basically stalking my work calls. Not Death. Nope.

I sighed, picking up one of the spell books. "Maybe he wasn't a ghost, but he was *something*. I see him all the time, Cassie. He was at a drowning a few days ago, standing off to the side and watching me. Then I swear I saw him when I was responding to a cardiac call. Then there was the griffin with pneumonia."

"But he wasn't at Silas Crabtree's tail emergency?" Casssie grinned.

"It's not funny," I protested. "No, he wasn't there when I was helping Silas. He's only there when it's critical, when it's a life-or-death kind of call."

"You're right, it's not funny. Sounds like some creepy guy who gets off on emergencies. He probably has a police scanner, listens for the call, then goes out to watch."

I frowned in thought. "Maybe, but the guy seems more focused on me then on the victim."

"So, he's got a first responder fetish? You've got yourself a stalker?"

Weirdo that I was, I kind of dug that idea. "No one else has seen him hanging around. No one else remembers seeing him at my calls, either."

"So, he's an invisible man? Only visible to you? And he's going to all the critical calls, but no one else realizes it because only you can see him."

This was getting ridiculous. "You don't believe in ghosts, but you believe in invisibility?"

Cassie shrugged. "Magical illusions. It's not a stretch."

"Except this is a *guy*, and men aren't witches," I countered. Only women inherited the ability to do magic. There were some instances where the son of a witch had some very minor skills, but not the sort of ability that significant illusions or invisibility would require. "Plus, if he did somehow manage to pull off an illusion that rendered him invisible, why was *I* able to see him?"

Cassie nodded. "Okay. I'm voting for creepy perv that only you somehow notice, but if you say ghost, then I'll believe you."

Death. I shook my head at the notion. Ghost seemed more acceptable.

"I don't know if it's a ghost or not," I told her. "I was hoping you'd have some idea on this. Well, an idea beyond creepy perv or the invisible man that only I can see."

"I could ask Lucien later tonight when he's back, but I think your best bet is to check with Babylon," Cassie told me.

"Where's Lucien that he won't be home until tonight?" That was a shocker. It was noon on a Saturday. I couldn't imagine what could tear the demon from Cassie's side for five or six hours.

"Work." She rolled her eyes. "He's got some business in the fifth circle of hell. I don't really want to know about it, so

I didn't ask for details. Ever since Bronwyn took up with Hadur, Lucien's been trying to spend some time in hell once or twice a week. Seems being called a spoiled, entitled, privileged brat by a warmonger stung a bit and he's trying to prove that he takes his infernal duties seriously."

Men. Made me glad I was single. Actually, it made me glad that when I did date, I tended toward nice normal human guys and not ones with horns or tails, or hellfire shooting from their eyeballs or something.

Suddenly my thoughts drifted to the man at the accident scenes. He was... well, he was damned hot, I'll admit that. What I'd seen lately was pretty drool-worthy. Thin, but in an elegant way with an easy stride that signaled a wiry strength. Angular features. Dark brown hair. Dark eyes. It was his eyes that really drew me in. They were intense. Not brooding, not emo, but intense. It was as if this man calmly watched the worst, remained steadfast in the face of a million crises. Here I was forcing back my panic at the thought of losing a patient, and he seemed to regard it all as if he held the very keys to life and death in his hands.

It was sexy—so very sexy. Cassie's demon boyfriend was hot, as in looked-like-he-stepped-out-of-a-magazine-spread hot. Bronwyn's demon boyfriend looked mountain-man-who-can-bench-press-a-Jeep hot. But this guy was *my* kind of hot. Unflappable. Calm. Collected. Confident.

I was a total weirdo in that I sort of wanted him to be a stalker, like Cassie said. Not because I particularly liked stalkers, but because that would mean he was coming to these calls to see me.

Would it be creepy for me to ask a man out on a date as I was loading a patient into the ambulance? Probably.

CHAPTER 3

OPHELIA

I stared into the murky depths of the water, willing it to reveal its secrets, to bring clarity to the disturbing visions that had been haunting my sleep lately. When the universe wants you to know something, it tells you. Except sometimes it tells you in crazy gibberish that's absolutely impossible to figure out.

Once more I'd had a restless night. Once more, the visions of blood had plagued me—faint blurry images, smells and sounds, a feeling of dread and doom, all of it an incomprehensible mishmash of nonsense. It was time for me to take the minotaur by the horns and figure this out before it drove me insane. It was time for me to attempt to divine exactly what these visions of blood meant.

All it took was a bowl of water and a spell. Well, in theory that's all it took. In reality, this might yield me nothing more than the gibberish of the dreams.

A trillion pathways converge and dissect, a tangled knot of thread.

Show me the one that will come to fruition. Show me the future ahead.

The water turned black as onyx, its surface like a mirror. I touched the edge of the bowl, running my finger around the rim as I repeated the spell. Vertigo sent my heart into my throat and my consciousness slipped forward into the shining dark water.

Blood on leaves. I reached out and touched their waxy green, feeling the thick stickiness of congealed red. Oleander. This was the blood of my dreams, I knew it. The oleander leaves were new. I pushed harder, wanting to know more. I couldn't warn someone, couldn't intervene to help if all I had to go on was blood that could be anyone's and some plant that could be anywhere.

The oleander dissolved into the inky blackness of the water and now I was on top of a mountain. A decision. Two courses of action, one which led to death, and the other to... death. Oh, great. *That* was helpful.

Mountain. A rocky peak where I could fall either forward or backward. I was so high I could nearly touch the moon. Its craggy surface seemed like divots on a golf ball.

Golf. Manicured greens and goblins with plaid shorts and berets with little fuzzy balls on top.

No. No, no, no. I was pretty sure golfing goblins had nothing to do with my vision. I needed to get back to the blood, back to the mountaintop. The blood was important. The decision on the mountain was important. Golfing goblins were most likely not important.

Blood. We were back to blood on the oleander leaves. Something smelled rancid. It was the heavy foul smell of death, of something that had lain in the open too long. A tree line. Underbrush. Oleanders parted, their branches moving aside to reveal the source of the smell.

I was afraid of what I might see. Death. A body. Terror roared through me and unable to face it, I shut my eyes.

When I opened them, the smell was gone and so was the tree line.

We were back to golf balls. I heard a voice and turned to see Marcus, the panther shifter, behind me.

"You did this," he scolded me. "It's your fault."

"What's my fault?" I asked him, full of dread.

Had I failed and someone was dead as a result? Dead and lying in the oleanders, in a pile of golf balls? What was my fault? What had I done wrong? And what choice would I make where death lay on either side?

I came out of the trance with a gasp, sweat trickling between my breasts. The bowl in front of me only held clear water. Before I could forget anything, I grabbed the pen and paper I'd placed by my side and wrote everything down. Then I got up and fixed myself a hot tea and tried to make sense of the whole thing.

I was a witch, an oracle, and my spells were a whole lot less clear and precise then those of my sisters. We all had our specialties, except for Cassie who was a bit of a witch generalist and also the most powerful of us all. My specialty was revealing the past, the present, and the future. Sometimes it was a useful gift, like when John, our resident cyclops, needed to find his car keys, or one of the leprechauns needed to know where his dearly departed great uncle Seamus had hidden his gold, or when the nymphs wanted to know when the first frost would be. That stuff was easy. The hard stuff was…well, hard.

Death. It was my nemesis and no matter how hard I tried, I couldn't seem to see the future when it came to the who, how, and when of death. Car keys, gold, and accurate weather prediction, yes. Death, no. Any vision having to do with death was so unclear, it was basically useless.

My first rare glimpse of a future fatality was when I was four. I'd woken up crying, babbling about falling, and how my chest hurt, and something about those fuzzy pipe cleaners kids use in school art projects. It was just a bad dream, Momma had told me. But when we were on our way to the grocery store that afternoon, a squirrel had fallen from a tree right onto our windshield. Momma had slammed on the breaks, throwing me forward.

My chest hurt from the seatbelt. The squirrel had died. Evidently something in my brain had interpreted "squirrel" as a fuzzy pipe cleaner. This was the sort of the weirdness that came with any divination. And this was the beginning of my life-long battle with death. Every vision that hinted at injury, sickness, fatality, was one I pursued with every fiber of my being, with every bit of my magical ability. If only I could figure out who, what, when, and how, then I could prevent it—I could save someone's life.

It never worked. No matter how hard I'd tried, I could never figure the visions out enough to prevent a death. Or even to figure out who it was that was going to die.

I'd become a paramedic. I was a first responder, fighting death with everything I had. And whenever I had visions of falling or blood and got that sense of doom, I tried my darnedest to learn enough that maybe one day I could use my magic to save someone's life. I see myself as less of a witch and more of a caped crusader with a pointy hat, throat-punching the grim reaper and stealing his victim from under his scythe.

Maybe this time, I could make a difference. Maybe I could figure out this vision and intervene. Maybe I could save a life.

Blood on oleander leaves. I poured my coconut oolong into a mug and mulled over the symbols in the vision. Oleanders were poisonous. Ingesting them caused severe gastric distress including seizures, coma, and death. Touching the leaves sometimes resulted in skin irritation. Even burning the things was a hazard since the smoke could also cause death.

But they were beautiful with their waxy, vivid green leaves. They bloomed from summer to fall, in a cluster of funnel-shaped blooms that could be white, pink, red, or yellow. The flowers symbolized love, but a love that should be approached with caution.

Love and death. Caution. Toxicity that could result in death. Hmmm.

The blood on the leaves made me think that the vision was emphasizing the death part, but blood could also mean love. Love that kills? Was the corpse I smelled at the tree line killed by a lover? In mythology, Leander died trying to swim to see his lover.

Mountaintop. Two choices. Moon. The moon and the mountaintop made me think of the shifters—especially the werewolves that were in the middle of a contentious division in their pack right now. There had been skirmishes, but so far, no out-and-out war. I'd tried to divine the future of that conflict but had come up with zeros. Was this vision telling me something about the werewolf pack? Was death coming to Heartbreak Mountain?

The symbols fit. And Marcus? Not only was he a panther shifter, but he was our prosecutor in the town of Accident. He was also my sister Cassie's ex-boyfriend.

In my divination, Marcus was accusing me of being at fault in something. It had been my fault, he'd said. Did that have to do with the terrible corpse-like smell of decay in the foliage by the trees? The very thought of my being at fault in someone's death, at my failing to save a life, made the tea curdle in my stomach. But was Marcus accusing me because of his role as our town's prosecutor? Or did he play a more personal and less symbolic role in this divination?

And did any of this have to do with the man I'd been

seeing on the most serious of my calls? The man who hovered on the edge of the scene, watching with an unnerving intensity. I couldn't help but think the two were somehow connected.

A mysterious man.

Blood on oleanders.

A choice on a mountaintop, of which either way lay death.

A panther shifter accusing me of…something.

And golf balls. I had no idea what the golf balls had to do with any of this. I was half tempted to discount them as a strange tangent of my weird witch-brain, but I'd learned long ago that it was the truly weird stuff that ended up being the key of most mysteries.

The fuzzy pipe cleaner had been a squirrel. What the heck were golf balls?

CHAPTER 4

OPHELIA

I took the stairs up to the third floor, bypassing the elevator in favor of getting some exercise. Pushing open the heavy door, I stood in a white carpeted hallway, flanked on one side by the elevator bays and on the other by tall glass doors with gold embossed lettering on them.

Prosecutors didn't normally have fancy offices in the closest thing Accident had for a high-rise professional building, but then most towns didn't have a panther shifter for a prosecutor.

Grabbing the brass handle, I swung one of the glass doors open and entered. Marcus' office was like a jungle. Hot. Humid. Chock full of plants. I could barely see the woman behind the desk from all the greenery. She stood, scooting a huge philodendron aside to greet me with a smile.

"Ophelia! What a pleasant surprise. Does Marcus know you were coming?"

I knew Ducha. I'd gone to high school with her but where I'd gone on to be a paramedic, she'd become a paralegal, working with Cassie for a little while at Tower and Mulkeefie. Where better for a hyena shifter to work then a law firm owned by two sphinxes? Last I'd heard, she was in her third year of law school. This gig with Marcus must be some sort of internship, although there was a good chance Ducha was angling for his job. Or thinking of eating him. Hyenas were like that.

"Is Marcus still the prosecutor, or did he suddenly decide to become a horticulturist?" I ducked under a hanging asparagus fern and wove my way through a maze of red veined prayer plants.

"I thought I'd spruce up the office a bit." She gave me a toothy smile. "Make the place a little homier."

Homey for her maybe. I'd seen what Marcus' office looked like a few years ago, and I'd been in his condo once or twice. The guy liked spartan living in high places. His decorative style was best described as geometric minimalist. I was surprised he'd let Ducha get away with this sort of thing. The panther shifter was no lightweight when it came to asserting himself, although Marcus tended to use charm and sex as his persuasion techniques and I wasn't sure how well that would work on a hyena shifter. Don't get me wrong. I'm pretty sure Ducha liked sex as much as anyone, but hyenas never let a good roll in the sheets cloud their judgement or their determination to have things their way.

"Well." I looked around, trying to think of something complimentary to say. "It's…lovely."

The hyena shifter beamed. "Of course it is. Now, is Marcus expecting you?"

"Nope." I stood there for a while and counted. One, two, three, four.

Ducha met the challenge, trying to stare me down. But where the hyena was going for dominance, I was simply standing my ground patiently. Finally, she laughed, reaching out to run her fingers across the fronds of something that looked like a small palm. "Go on in. I won't even warn him because I like the way you roll, Ophelia. Always have."

"Back at 'cha, Ducha." I gave her a quick salute, then slowly made my way through the mini forest, thinking that next time I'd need to bring a machete. Clear of the shrubberies, I went down a short hallway that led to the huge glass-walled conference room that doubled as Marcus' office.

Marcus looked up at me as I entered, then shot an irritated glance over my shoulder. "Clearly I need to have a discussion about job duties with my intern."

"Be careful. I think she bites," I warned him. Actually, I knew Ducha bit. Several of our town residents bore the scars. And yes, every one of the bitten had deserved them.

The panther shifter's eyelids drooped, turning the irritated glance into one of pure sex. "So do I," he purred.

I caught my breath, knowing full well why Cassie had stayed with this guy and put up with his philandering ways for so long.

Turning down the seduction a few notches, Marcus shifted in his seat and suddenly became every bit the serious, professional town prosecutor. Don't get me wrong, this hot-lawyerly dude he'd suddenly become was still…well, hot, but in a different way then panther-shifter-with-the-sex-drive-of-a-porno-character hot.

"So, what can I do for you, Ophelia?"

His voice still purred, and I steeled myself against his charm, plopping down in the chair across from his desk. He'd done this even when he'd been dating Cassie. It had been weird knowing that your sister's boyfriend would happily boink you and your other sisters—either individually or all together. It wouldn't have meant anything to Marcus. It wouldn't have changed how he felt about Cassie. For panther shifters, sex was sex, and relationships were relationships. It had been something Cassie had always struggled to reconcile herself with, and eventually she'd issued an ultimatum which Marcus, to his credit, had tried to comply with.

Tried and failed. Which was just as well because Sunday family dinners were a whole lot easier without constantly being propositioned by your sister's boyfriend.

But this was hopefully all water under the bridge. I was here for a reason, and it had nothing to do with Marcus bending me over his desk and screwing my brains out.

"I been having dreams, so I did a divination spell and you were in the vision."

Suddenly every bit of sexual tension evaporated from the room. Marcus clenched his jaw and let out a slow measured breath. "Me?"

No one wanted to be in my visions. My eldest sister may have been named Cassandra, but I was the one who'd become the prophetess of doom, not her. Finding keys and predicting weather was fine, but people got uncomfortable around oracles. Everyone says they want to know the future, but when it comes down to it, they don't. Nobody wants to know they're going to be hurt in a terrible car accident, or that their wife is going to run off with her co-worker, or that their friend is going to steal money from their wallet.

Nobody wants to know when and how they're going to die.

None of my visions or divinations had revealed that sort of detail, but that fact didn't stop people from being a bit afraid of me and what I might tell them one day. Marcus was clearly terrified that I was here to inform him that he'd drown next Tuesday or be crushed by a falling piano or eaten by his hyena intern.

"In the vision, I saw blood and smelled something dead over by a tree line—not you, though. You weren't bloody or dead," I told him hastily, seeing his eyes widen. "I didn't actually see a corpse; I just smelled one. And there was blood on

27

oleander leaves, a mountaintop with a choice, and the moon…and golf balls."

His eyebrows shot up. "Golf balls? As in golf ball golf balls?"

I nodded. "Golf ball golf balls."

"Witches," he muttered. I thought I caught a note of regret in the word, and it made me wonder if he was still harboring some feelings for my sister. "You're all crazy," he continued.

Okay, maybe it wasn't regret after all.

"Probably, but I don't know if golf balls are significant. I think I saw them because I was looking at the moon and imagining that with the craters and how it looked like a big golf ball in the sky, then suddenly there were golf balls, and goblins in plaid shorts on the fairway. Maybe that's significant—a symbol of something important—or maybe just my weird brain intruding on the vision."

"Or maybe the dead guy got hit in the head with a golf ball and bled on the oleander leaves while playing the back nine at night on a mountaintop course," Marcus suggested.

That sounded pretty improbable to me, but maybe he was right. Sometimes a golf ball was just a golf ball.

"Where do I play into this vision?" Marcus asked, shifting uneasily in his chair as he clearly contemplated what horror I was about to reveal.

"I was looking down at where the corpse smell was coming from, at the blood on the oleander leaves, and…" I hesitated for dramatic impact. Yeah, I know it was mean, but Marcus deserved a little moment of anxiety for his constant cheating on my sister. "You were suddenly behind me. You told me that it was my fault. You were really annoyed at me about it. I got the impression that I'd done something and because of that, maybe someone was dead?"

Marcus leaned back in his chair, visibly relieved. "That's it? I didn't explode or burst into flames or anything?"

"Nope."

"I wasn't dead on the grass, bleeding out on the oleander leaves?"

"Nope."

"I wasn't getting stabbed in the back by a jealous husband while I was screwing his wife?"

Oh, I was so tempted to reply in the affirmative to that one, but honesty prevailed. "Nope."

Marcus was silent a few moments, no doubt contemplating his enjoyment of life and wondering if this counted as one of his nine lives.

Panther shifters didn't really have nine lives—at least as far as I knew.

"I don't have any cases concerning dead bodies or an assault amid a bunch of oleander bushes," he finally told me. "Sheriff Oakes briefs me weekly on open cases just so I know what might be coming my way, and he hasn't said anything about an attack, or a murder or wrongful death investigation. Maybe my presence in the vision is symbolic, as the voice of the law? As a social accuser?"

"I thought about that but wanted to see if any of that rang a bell and if you could provide any insights that might help me interpret the vision."

"Moon and mountaintop, plus a stinky corpse in a wooded area makes me think of the werewolf conflict," he commented. "Although the pack has always been self-governing in the past, with Cassie taking her rightful role, we may be tasked with applying more and more of the laws of Accident to the pack."

Cassie had pondered doing just that. It bothered her that in the past fights for dominance and territory, what had been unlawful murders had been covered up under the guise of challenges to the death. She wanted to outlaw those types of challenges as well as the death penalties that the pack considered part of their culture and have all legal matters within the werewolf pack be subject to the laws of Accident. Lucien had vowed to back her up on this, but she'd decided on a course of slow, purposeful changes instead.

"I talked to Cassie the other night, and although she's making every attempt to come to a diplomatic solution to the werewolf problem, it might end up being war," I admitted.

Marcus shrugged. "Then there's your corpse in the woods, and your mountain, and your moon. My interpretation is to stay off the mountain or risk stumbling over a dead werewolf."

It made absolute sense, but visions didn't adhere to Occam's Razor. The easiest interpretation was quite frequently the wrong one.

"So then what do you have to do with any of this? Or golf balls?"

"Maybe the universe is telling you to take up golf." He sent a smoldering glance my way. "And to let me take you home and not leave my bed until morning."

Again, I had an image of myself bent over his desk while he drove into me from behind. Two things were wrong with that very tempting idea, though. One, I wasn't into a "just sex" encounter. Two, this man was my sister's ex-boyfriend and thus completely off the menu as far as I was concerned.

"Maybe the universe is telling me to pick up a nine iron and drive some golf balls up your ass." I smirked, because of all the people in Accident, I knew Marcus had enough ego to not take offense at my joking threat.

He wiggled his eyebrows. "Might be fun. Give me a call, Ophelia. I'll bring both the nine iron *and* I'll bring the balls."

Remind me never to spar verbally with a panther shifter.

I got up to leave, only to stop dead by the door, staring at the plant on a bookshelf—a plant I hadn't seen when I came in. Marcus' office was typically spartan, neutral in color and full of sharp angles. But here was a plant with glossy leaves and clustered flowers.

Oleander.

My eyesight narrowed and red liquid welled on the stems, blood rolling down the leaves and leaving streaks of red behind as it dropped to the floor with a soft splat. A dark road. The foul smell of a rotting corpse. A moon breaking free from the clouds. But this time it wasn't Marcus behind me; it was the man from the accident scenes. His presence felt heavy like a suffocating blanket, like the finality of the grave. His dark eyes held mine and he spoke, but *his* words weren't of blame.

"Choose," he commanded in a whispered voice. "A life for a life. Choose."

"Stupid plant."

Marcus' voice jolted me out of the vision with such speed that I felt disoriented and suddenly cold.

"Darn Ducha and her plants. I told her I didn't want any of those things in here," he continued.

I picked it up, running my fingers across the bright blue pebbled surface of the pot, then touching the leaves that were so very toxic.

"Take it," Marcus urged. "And take a few of the ones out in the lobby as well. Actually, pull up a box truck and take them all and Ducha with them. That woman's going to be the death of me."

Suddenly I got a vision, a flash of insight. And I smiled, because Ducha *was* going to be the death of Marcus, just not the sort of death he was thinking.

I left without saying a word about the vision. And yes, I took the plant.

CHAPTER 5

OPHELIA

I headed home, taking the twisty country lanes that ran through the valley meadows and farms. Cassie and three of my other sisters lived inside the actual town of Accident. West of town lay forests and streams, and a break in the mountain range that led past the town wards to the outside world. The mountains loomed large, curling around the town on three sides like a "C." The rest of the area was rolling countryside, spacious and far larger than it seemed when up high and looking down into the valley below. Originally the founder of the town, my ancestor Temperance Perkins, had only included the town proper within the magical wards that protected the supernatural residents from discovery, but over the centuries the wards had been expanded to encompass fields and streams, farms and forests, mountain and valley.

I lived out to the east where the opening in the "C" of mountains lay. Something eased in my soul to be out from under the shadow of the rocky crags, in the place where minotaur and unicorns grazed. So many of our citizens liked the wide open fields, and I loved living among the centaurs, the Pegasus, and the manticores. At the far eastern edge of what we claimed to be part of Accident was Pottsmore Bay, a small inlet whose water was just brackish enough that the merfolk and selkies called it home. Let others live among the trolls and the shifters and the fae. These open fields and watery marshes were what I liked to called home.

My house was just west of where the merfolk lived, in a cluster of houses we'd taken to calling Pottsmore after the bay. Creative, I know. About forty of us lived here, each in wood-sided homes built on stilts to guard against the occasional flood. I loved it here. The only time I regretted not being closer to town was when I had to work.

Which was tonight. I glanced at my watch, realizing that I'd only have about four hours to grab a quick nap, shower, eat, then head back to town for my shift at the fire department. Hopefully it would be a slow night and I could grab a few more hours of sleep, but the Accident Fire Department had the dubious honor of responding to calls outside of our wards and into the human world. There was a good chance I'd be swamped, especially since it was Saturday night and weekends didn't mix well with twisty mountain roads.

Turning onto the one-lane bridge that crossed the estuary and led to Pottsmore, I happened to glance over the railing to see something floating in the water. At first, I thought it was a buoy for a crab pot, but then I realized it wasn't.

I slammed on the brakes, leaving my door open as I jumped out of the car and scrambled over the low railing, dropping myself down into the water. It was cold and murky, full of marsh grass and floating plant life. I surfaced with tendrils of yellowish green clinging to my hair, the smell of salt and fish and silt filling my nose. Grabbing the small form, I turned him over and swam for the shore, praying the whole way.

Hauling him up onto the soft muddy ground, I checked

for vitals. With a sinking heart, I cleared his airway and began CPR.

My phone. Damn it, I'd left my phone in the passenger seat of my car in my haste to get to this guy. Which was probably just as well since having a non-functioning water-laden cell phone would do me just as much good right now as a phone all the way up on the bridge. As I shifted to begin chest compressions, I hoped that someone would be driving in or out of Pottsmore, would see my car sitting in the middle of the bridge with the driver's door open, and come to see what was going on.

I'd just started round two when I saw movement out of the corner of my eye. Tilting my head a bit, I saw someone—just legs from my angle, but still someone.

"Call 911," I told him or her as I moved back to chest compressions. "Tell them I've got a goblin drowning on the east side of the bridge into Pottsmore."

Goblins. Incredibly hearty creatures, but they really were idiots when it came to water. All efforts to teach them to swim failed. If they'd just remember to roll over and float on their backs, they'd be fine, but no. Every time they fell into the water or just wandered in over their heads, they panicked and flailed around, sinking like a stone and only bobbing to the surface after they'd gotten their lungs full of water. If this had been a human, I wouldn't have held out much hope, but we'd managed to pull six goblins back from the edge of a drowning death this year. I was determined to make this one number seven.

"You're too late."

The voice sent a chill through me and I looked up to see the same man from the accident scenes. My heart thudded with a combination of attraction and unease.

"I'm never too late," I lied. Or maybe it wasn't really a lie, but some attempt at confidence in god-like abilities I didn't possess. "Fake it until you make it" didn't ever work for me, but I was willing to give it a try.

"His soul is separating. He will soon move on."

One. Two. Three. Four. I continued my chest compressions, then checked vitals again. Nothing. Even if my buddies teleported here with the ambulance, they wouldn't be in time. This could be our first goblin fatality this year. I smoothed a hand over his warty, green head and started to cry as I continued to work on the goblin.

Why had I not had a vision about *this* instead of stupid golf balls and blood on oleander leaves? If I'd left Marcus' just a few minutes earlier, if I'd not stopped to get gas, if I'd just driven faster, this little guy would be alive and ready to terrorize town residents for another few years. What use was it being an oracle if I couldn't *save* anyone?

"Don't cry, darling. Don't cry."

I felt the man's hand on my shoulders and looked over. At first glance, the hand seemed bony, almost skeletal. Then suddenly it was firm with long slender fingers, muscled, and covered with tanned flesh.

The goblin coughed, vomiting up water and lunch all over himself. His eyelids opened, and the viscous cloudiness of death cleared from his bulbous eyes like the mists on a sunny day, revealing brown irises.

"A life for a life," the man whispered, and I shivered as I remembered the vision in Marcus' office. "Soon you must make a choice."

He turned to walk away, and I stood, leaving the goblin spitting and babbling something about tasty fishies as he lay in the mud.

"Who are you?" I asked, rushing up to the man. "I mean, you said you were Death, but I can't exactly call you that so I was hoping you'd have an actual name. And that maybe you'd like to go get coffee sometime? Or dinner?"

Had I just asked Death out on a date? No, he wasn't Death; he was a ghost. Although I wasn't sure it was any better that I'd just asked a ghost out on a date.

Could ghosts have sex? Maybe I shouldn't be thinking about that. I mean, it wasn't like he'd said yes to my coffee invite or done anything except turn and stare at me with those dark, expressionless eyes.

"I am Nirnasha."

And with that, he was gone, leaving me staring out into the marshes, a coughing goblin behind me.

CHAPTER 6

OPHELIA

"No one needs my help. No one ever comes to *me* for help. Noooo. It's always Cassie, or Bronwyn, or you, or Glenda. Not me." Babylon poured me a cup of coffee and plopped it down in front of me. Then she flounced over in her yoga pants and sports bra to get one for herself.

I'd skipped sleep, opting instead for a quick shower, take out, and a visit with my youngest sister before I headed in to work. Maybe Cassie was right. Maybe Babylon would be able to shed some light on who this mysterious—and mysteriously hot—man was that kept showing up at scenes of death. And near death.

"So, you and Adrienne and Sylvie all get together and have pity parties?" I teased. "The sisters with weird magic that freak everyone out."

She scowled, sitting down next to me with her cup of coffee. "Sylvie can't come to the pity party. Everyone likes a luck witch. It's Addie and I that are the black sheep of the family."

I reached out and tugged on a strand of Lonnie's red hair

37

that had escaped her messy topknot. "Well, I'm here now. Guess I'll need to figure out a reason to ask Adrienne for help so she doesn't feel left out. Maybe I'll have her call more bluebirds to my feeder or something."

Adrienne communicated with animals, and they eagerly did her bidding. Most of the time anyway. Of the pair of them, Babylon had the weirdest magic, though. Necromancy. No one in our family going back to when Temperance Perkins escaped the pyre and founded our town had ever been skilled in necromancy. The closest had been that aunt back in the eighteenth century who was a medium. The unusual and scary magical ability had always made Lonnie feel like an outcast. Even though Dad had taken off on us before she'd been born, she'd always felt that was somehow her fault. It was bullshit. She'd had nothing to do with dad leaving. She'd had nothing to do with Momma's leaving either.

Although having a baby animate a spider you'd just squashed *was* a bit unnerving.

Babylon shifted in her seat, cradling her coffee in her hands. She'd gotten our father's auburn hair, but unlike Cassie and Bronwyn who had reddish brown locks, Lonnie's hair was bright fire-engine red. Even with her light complexion and freckled skin, she was a few shades tanner than my deathly pale, though. Like Sylvie and I, she'd gotten the rare blue eyes, except hers were a dark stormy gray-blue where mine and my twin's looked practically neon.

"So, what do you know about ghosts?" I asked, getting right to the topic.

"Pretty much nothing." Lonnie sipped her coffee. "You'd think I'd have some means of communicating with the dead, but no. All I get is their bodies. Lovely, huh?"

Did all youngest siblings complain this much? Sheesh.

"Cassie said you could do something where a spirit straddled both worlds, partially in their reanimated body and partially in the afterlife, so you've got to have *some* means of communication with them," I countered.

She grimaced. "That was a mistake. Even if I could replicate it, I wouldn't want to. Yes, that undead had more autonomy and was less of a drain on my magic, but I could hear him, Ophelia. I could hear his voice in my head. I couldn't get him to shut up about the guy who killed him, or the 2011 World Series, or what he had for dinner the night before. If I had to listen to him wax poetic about that damned shrimp scampi one more time, I was going to shoot myself."

"So, you let him go?" I looked around, worried that I was going to find some shambling zombie in the hallway.

"Of course I let him go. I can't reanimate for more than a few hours, especially something the size of a human. I didn't even want to spend a few hours with that guy and his shrimp scampi story, so I let him go right away."

I could tell that despite her light tone that she wasn't joking. The experience had unnerved my sister. It took a lot to shake Babylon. Someone who had been able to raise the dead since infancy wasn't a witch who was easily spooked.

"You okay?" I eyed her with concern. "Have you reanimated anything since then? Was it a one-time occurrence, you think?"

She took a long drink of coffee and didn't meet my eyes. "It's fine. I'm fine. Next time I'll stick to raising road kill, or something that isn't obsessed with his fine dining choices."

"Why do you even do it, Lonnie?" We'd had this discussion a million times and she'd never given me or any of us a straight answer. "Unless you're trying to raise an army to defeat an evil overlord, or it's Halloween, I don't see any reason to go messing with the dead."

"It's what I do. Now stop being freaked out about my

magical talent and tell me about this ghost you think you saw."

I repeated the story about seeing the man at the various calls, how he seemed to be watching me, how he vanished seemingly into thin air, how no one besides me had noticed him.

"But not all your calls?" Lonnie asked. "He didn't show up at Silas Crabtree's tail emergency? Or the anxiety attack one? Or the gnome kid with the croup?"

I shook my head. "He's at the serious ones—ones where I'm normally too busy trying to keep someone alive to go ask him why he keeps showing up. Once I asked him who he was, and he told me Death. Then this afternoon, when I was pretty sure that goblin had drowned, he told me his name was Nirnasha right after I asked him out to dinner. Or coffee."

Lonnie made a strangled sound. "You asked someone who could be a ghost or a weirdo stalker out to dinner?"

I shrugged. "He's hot. At first, he had this sort of silent-dude-in-robes appeal, but now he wears a suit and you know how I like men in suits. Plus, it's not like he's a skeleton, or a wraith, or walks around wearing a hockey mask or anything."

"You're so weird." Lonnie shook her head.

"Oh, like you're normal," I shot back. None of us were normal. I wasn't sure if it was because we were witches or because we were just a bunch of weirdos, but we all had some strange quirks going on.

"So, what do *you* think?" I asked.

"I think he's a reaper," Lonnie replied.

I blinked. "A what? You mean the specter of death? So you believe he really *was* serious when he said he was Death?"

"No, not exactly *Death*. A reaper. They come to collect the souls of the dead."

"So how is that not Death?"

Lonnie gave me the look. It was the look she gave any of us when she felt we were being particularly dense.

"Reapers don't kill. They just show up when someone's going to die and help free their soul. It's not the same thing. Trust me."

Sounded like the same thing to me. "And you've seen these things?"

Lonnie shivered. "Occasionally. Usually when I'm doing my magic, the reaper has been long gone. I have run across a few though. It's best to stand back and let them do their thing before you go trying to raise the dead. Actually, it's best to come back when someone's been dead a few days and you're sure. They're scary mofos, Ophelia. Scary."

"I don't think it's a reaper, Lonnie."

She arched an eyebrow. "He appears at the calls where someone dies? When you lose the patient?"

I thought back. "I haven't lost a patient in the last month, but it was definitely a possibility at those calls where he shows up."

"Dude wears a cape?"

"A cape?" I snorted. "Do you seriously think I'd ask a man in a freaking *cape* to dinner? I told you, it was robes at first, but now it's a suit." I felt my cheeks heat up. "He's good look-ing. Really good looking. Not the sort of guy Cassie or Wynnie would go for, but definitely my type."

"Thin but muscled. Elegant and poised. Cool and confi-dent." Lonnie grinned, clearly knowing my type.

"Yep."

"I think it's a reaper who is waiting in the wings to see if he's needed or not."

I wrinkled my nose. "Seriously? You think they'd know that. Whether someone's going to die or not, I mean."

She shrugged. "I can't imagine it's all that easy with

41

modern medical technology. We can pretty much bring people back from the brink of death, save people who would have been considered dead just fifty years ago. I doubt reapers can see the future, that they're oracles like you are. Maybe they appear, thinking someone's going to die, only to go back empty handed sometimes."

"Well, that's a shitty kind of job," I told her. "Having to race all over the place for near-death experiences where you might not be needed after all. That sucks. It would be more efficient if they waited and got the call *after* someone had actually died. It can't be all that horrible to have a newly dead spirit hanging around their body for ten minutes or so while a reaper arrives. Would save a lot of time if they were sure dead was dead first."

Lonnie snorted. "I'll pass along your efficiency suggestions the next time I see a reaper. Which hopefully will be never."

I frowned in thought. "If he's a reaper, he's not reaping a lot of souls. At least not on my watch in the last few months. Maybe he's not a reaper, but a kind of guardian angel, sent to protect these people who are near death?"

Lonnie laughed. "Okay, now I'm envisioning some epic smack down between a reaper and an angel, both duking it out over whether someone dies or not."

"Seriously," I urged. "We've got two demons living in Accident. Who's to say there isn't an angel lurking around?"

My sister pursed her lips. "Maybe. Some people think reapers actually *are* angels—angels of death. I've never met an angel, so I don't know."

"An angel of death or a guardian angel?" I mused. "Let me tell you, the odds are really against some of these patients, especially that goblin this afternoon. That goblin should never have survived outside of some kind of divine intervention. Yep. He's a guardian angel. A gorgeous, hot, guardian angel that I'd love to get naked."

"You're so going to get zapped by a bolt of lightning," Lonnie teased.

"So says the woman who animates dead things," I shot back with a grin.

She shook her head and sipped her coffee. Then she shrugged. "Okay. Let's say he *is* a guardian angel. If so, he seems to be selective about who he's saving because I've seen plenty of obituaries in the county this past month. Maybe he's only saving your patients as a sort of gift. Like when a cat brings you a dead mouse or something."

I thought about that a moment, feeling rather flustered at the direction my ideas were heading.

"Maybe he's got a crush on you," Lonnie added, her thinking clearly running parallel with mine. "Maybe this angel thinks you're hot and he's trying to get in your pants by saving your patients."

Wow. Visual, there. Although the idea of me naked and sweaty, riding an angel for all he was worth seemed a bit sacrilegious.

"Or maybe he's a reaper with a crush on me who is trying to get in my pants by holding off on collecting souls." I watched my sister carefully and grinned to see her shudder.

"Ewww. Screwing a reaper. That's disgusting, Ophelia. Better hope it's an angel, because the thought of you doing a reaper is freaking me out here."

I laughed and finished my coffee. Reaper or angel. Either way, I needed to somehow try to have an actual conversation with this guy the next time he showed up. I'd gotten his name, but I never did get a reply to my dinner invitation. Yes, the next time I saw him, I was definitely going to repeat my date invitation, as weird as that sounded.

How I was going to accomplish that *was* a bit of a puzzle.

I could hardly abandon a critical patient to go chat up a hot reaper. He tended to vanish as soon as the patient was stable and I had a minute free, though. There had to be a way I could get in a word before he poofed off. There had to be some way I could make him stay so I could figure out who he was and what his intentions were.

But first, I probably had to decide what *my* intentions were. Could I date a reaper? Have a reaper boyfriend? What about my incredible fears of mortality? Those fears seemed a bit incompatible with the idea of dating Death, but crazy as I was, I was willing to give it a shot.

CHAPTER 7

OPHELIA

"Cassie? Why is there...hair? I don't know what this is, but I'm thinking it's hair. Why is there a bundle of hair on the table?"

I didn't always make it to Sunday night dinner at our family home. That was the price I paid for being a first responder. Occasionally I was at the station while everyone else ate pot roast or lasagna or pork tenderloin. This weekend I was lucky. I'd pulled a long, surprisingly boring shift last night and was actually off work for once. Eager for some family time, I'd arrived early with a green bean casserole that needed to go in the oven and found...this.

My eldest sister walked in from the kitchen, munching on a carrot stick, her long auburn hair in a pony tail. "It's a beard."

That wasn't the most enlightening of statements. "Okay, then. Why is there a beard on the table?" I looked closer. "Is it singed? Like from a fire?"

All my sisters were a little odd, but I couldn't imagine why Cassie would be carrying around a beard. It's not like any of us did curses. Well, Sylvie *could* do curses. It was the flip side of being a luck witch. Although Sylvie didn't like anyone to know about that particular skill, and as far as I knew, she'd never actually performed a curse besides that one in the third grade involving Mrs. Ingram's pencils. I couldn't imagine that this thing would be for a spell, especially since a curse only required one hair and not an entire beard.

"It's Clinton Dickskin's beard." Cassie munched on the carrot. "I burned it off his face."

First, ewww. "Cassie, we *eat* on this table. I'm not eating baked ziti on the same table that once held Clinton Dickskin's beard. Get it off. And get some bleach so I can sanitize everything."

She picked up the beard and held it aloft, considering it as if she were eyeing a work of art. "I'm trying to decide what to do with it."

"How about throw it in the trash?" I wrinkled my nose, wondering if I'd be able to eat anything at all tonight after this gruesome sight. I saw terribly injured bodies every day but coming across Clinton Dickskin's beard on our family dining room table had completely destroyed my appetite.

"I might frame it," Cassie mused. "Maybe get one of those shadowbox things."

Most people would be just as concerned about the fact that my sister burned a beard off some guy's face as the fact that it was lying on our table. Actually, most people would be *more* concerned about that.

I wasn't most people. And I completely understood why my sister would have burned the beard off a guy's face. Clinton Dickskin wasn't just any guy; he was a werewolf. *And* he was the werewolf who'd had the brakes cut in my sister Bronwyn's truck. Luckily, she'd just suffered some cuts and bruises and a broken leg, but she could have died.

She could have died. The remembrance sent a wave of cold through me.

"I'm surprised Clinton's head isn't on a pike out front of the house," I told Cassie.

She looked appalled. "Ophelia! We don't do capital punishment in Accident. Well, not without a trial, appropriate sentencing, and several opportunities for appeal."

No, we didn't do capital punishment, at least not in the last fifty years or so. We *did* evidently burn the beards off werewolves' faces, though. My eldest sister had a bit of a thing with fire. The story about Marcus' pants was a legend in town. On fire. In the middle of the courthouse. During closing arguments. I'm not saying he didn't deserve it, but Cassie's idea of justice was a little quirky, just like the town of Accident.

"We prosecuted the wolf that tampered with Bronwyn's truck and the ones who attacked her and Hadur at the cabin, Clinton paid for a new truck, trailer, and the tools that were lost or destroyed, and I burned off his beard a couple of weeks ago in a fit of temper which got me a stern lecture at my anger management meeting."

My sister had to attend court-mandated anger management meetings because of the prior "incident" involving Marcus' pants. I had a feeling she'd be attending those for the rest of her life.

"I'll admit I *was* tempted to take his head off." Cassie glared at the beard in her hand. "That's what Lucien wanted to do."

I shivered, remembering when we'd seen Bronwyn's mangled wreck of a truck, the trailer a twisted heap of metal behind it. The six of us had scrambled down that cliff, our hearts pounding, scared of what we might find when we got to the truck. I'd truly expected to find my sister dead in that cab. It had been the most terrifying experience of my life. I loved my sisters more than anything in the world. They were all I had. They were my everything.

Which was probably why I didn't date much. I loved my job. I loved my family. They both came first, and prior boyfriends hadn't been all that happy about playing third fiddle to the two other loves of my life.

Well, that and the whole witch thing. I preferred human guys, and human guys were in short supply in Accident. If I'd wanted to date a merman, or a gnome, or a vampire, or an elf, or a shifter, I would have been set. But human? Human men? Yeah, I had a choice of about five eligible bachelors and two of them were gay.

So, I tended to date outside of Accident, where humans didn't believe in magic or the supernatural creatures that roamed my town. If they entered town limits and saw the residents, they'd promptly forget about them after they left. That's what the wards around our town did—they kept us safe from persecution from the outside world. They provided a haven where we could all be ourselves without fear of being burned at the stake or shot with silver bullets or staked in a coffin. So, my dates never even knew what they were playing third fiddle to.

Let's just say that having to keep a major part of your life a secret from your boyfriend didn't make for a good relationship.

"Where *is* Lucien anyway?" I asked.

"I sent him to pick up ice cream. Men in the kitchen are guaranteed to be standing in front of every drawer or cabinet you need to get into. He was driving me crazy." It was all said with a smile and a besotted tone of voice that let me know what sort of crazy Lucien was causing.

"Can't cook with a sexy demon trying to get in your pants?" I asked.

She laughed. "Well, yeah. That too. He's been spending

more time in hell doing his job—which I definitely don't want to know the details of. I actually like it. I'm at work. He's at work. We see each other in the evenings, and then we screw like we've been apart for years."

"Ah, the honeymoon phase," I teased. "I guess you won't be needing Sylvie's services anytime soon."

My twin was a therapist and a life coach specializing in relationship counselling—*and* specializing in people's sex lives. Like Doctor Ruth, only with a pointy hat and a bunch of charms.

I was kidding. My twin didn't wear a pointy hat. She favored a jaunty beret on occasion, but no pointy hats.

"Heck no," Cassie replied. "Sylvie would have us tying each other up, and shoving household objects into various orifices with a generous application of lube, then composing poems to each other."

"Sounds like fun." Actually, it didn't sound like fun, but I loved to tease my eldest sister.

"Lucien would definitely think so, well, except for the poetry thing. Me? Not so much."

Cassie was turning an interesting shade of red that told me she was lying. I was betting that not only did those ideas appeal to her, but that she and Lucien had probably already tried them out. I wasn't able to pry any further details from her, though, as my other sisters and my cousin Aaron had arrived.

"Not the only guy anymore, huh?" I asked my cousin. Male witches weren't common, and they didn't usually have much, if any, magical ability. Aaron was older than all of us, but we'd always fawned over him, spoiling him as our only living male relative for as long as I could remember. He came to family dinners, borrowed stuff from us, called to ask us favors, and showed up randomly to chat or watch football. It was like having a little brother who was older in years, if that made any sense.

"You women can't gang up and pick on me anymore," he said with a smug expression. "I've got backup."

"Right. Lucien is going to side with Cassie over you, so don't get your hopes up, buddy."

Hadur might back him up, though. He'd do anything for Bronwyn, but from what I'd seen, he and Lucien had some history and their relationship with each other was on the prickly side—which would make our dinner tonight extra exciting. This was the first Sunday since we'd managed to spring Hadur from the summoning circle he'd been trapped in for two hundred years. I hoped Cassie had the foresight to seat him and Lucien at opposite ends of the table, or none of us might be enjoying our baked ziti tonight.

I turned from Aaron and saw Bronwyn walk in. Hadur was right behind her, his hand placed protectively on her lower back, his shoulder so close that it brushed hers. She'd only been off her crutches a short while and seeing her careful gait as she made her way across the room brought tears to my eyes.

"Wynnie!" I went to her, gently giving her a hug and kissing her cheek. Everyone else did the same until she was surrounded by six sisters and Aaron, all of us making a huge fuss of her.

She could have died. When I'd seen that car.... Yes, my divination had said she was alive and safe, but seeing that car had made me doubt my vision. It had sent icy cold fingers of fear through me. I couldn't lose her. I couldn't lose any of them. We were all we had. We were family. And the thought that one of us might die was more than I could bear.

"Hadur. It's so good to see you again," I told the demon. He'd pulled Bronwyn from the car, taken care of her, done more to heal her than I had done, than Glenda's smoothies had done. There was not a doubt in my mind that he loved her, and she just glowed when she was with him.

"Uh, thanks. You, too…"

I bit back a smile, realizing he was struggling to remember our names—and struggling to tell me apart from my twin.

"Ophelia."

He grimaced. "Right. Ophelia. The one who heals but doesn't heal. You're the oracle, correct?"

I nodded. "So now that you're a free demon, what are you enjoying the most?" I noted his quick glance at Bronwyn and quickly amended my question. "Besides sex with my sister."

He laughed at that. I got the idea that laughing was a new thing for him, and something he'd been doing more of in the past month than he ever had in his very long life.

"Oh, let's see…. Microwaves. Coffeemakers. The internet. Indoor plumbing. Bronwyn is teaching me to drive."

Now that had *me* laughing. "I'm surprised she lets anyone behind the wheel."

"Oh, I'm not teaching him with my new truck," Bronwyn said. "I borrowed John's car for the lessons."

"John the cyclops?" Yes, John the cyclops had no last name. He liked it that way. Quite a few of the supernatural residents of Accident were the same.

"Yes." She laughed. "John's got more dents in that thing than I have fingers and toes. I guess it's a hazard of not having any depth perception. He said a few more scrapes wouldn't matter, so it's the perfect driver's ed car for a warmonger. We're taking John out for dinner next week as a thank you."

"I like John," Hadur spoke up. "He expresses his anger very openly and doesn't let such emotions remain bottled up. It's good to see someone with such a healthy relationship with their rage."

I grimaced, thinking that most of Accident didn't agree with the demon's assessment. John the cyclops was constantly blowing his stack over things like litter, shopping carts not put back into the corral at the grocery store, and typos on Facebook posts. I wasn't alone in wishing the cyclops would bottle up his rage a bit more.

"Well, here's someone else you'll like." I pulled my cousin forward. "This is Aaron. He's our first cousin, but like a brother to us. And he's hoping you'll stick up for him when the sisterly teasing gets too much."

The two shook hands and I left them to whatever a male demon and a male witch would find to talk about while I helped Bronwyn to a chair then headed into the kitchen to assist Cassie. Lucien appeared with half-gallons of various flavors of ice cream, which he shoved into the freezer just as Cassie was pulling the baked ziti out of the oven. We all sat down and ate, the demons managing to ignore each other while the rest of us engaged in our usual lively conversation. After dinner, Aaron and Glenda cleared the table while Babylon roped Hadur into helping her with the ice cream. No one could decide what flavor they wanted, so we ended up just putting the tubs in the middle of the table, and we all did a circuit, putting a spoonful of each into our bowls. Lucien teased Cassie about saving some for later to lick off her body. Sylvie nodded in approval, saying that ice cream might be a bit too cold and that he should try whipped cream and chocolate syrup instead.

"Oh, that reminds me! There's fudge topping," Cassie exclaimed, scooting her chair back.

"I'll get it." Sylvie waved at her to stay seated. "Should I heat it up?"

"Just pop it in the microwave," Cassie called after her.

"Screw the hot fudge. I'm not waiting," Bronwyn announced, digging into her ice cream.

The next minute was a blur, stretched out and abnormally long as time gets when something causes adrenaline and fear to shoot through your system. I remembered tasting the cold creamy bite of ice cream, hearing the slam of the microwave door, the beep of the buttons, and the hum.

Then the explosion.

It started with a pop noise, then a bang and the sound of twisting metal. The air smelled hot, like melted plastic and burned chocolate. I didn't hear Sylvie scream or shriek or yelp. I didn't hear her say anything at all, and that frightened me more than the explosion.

Shoving my seat back so hard it fell, I ran for the kitchen, clearing the doorway before my chair crashed on the floor. Everyone else had sat frozen in surprise, but my movement got them going and soon the lot of them were up and racing after me. What I saw when I entered the kitchen made my breath catch. The microwave was smoking, flames along the back, sparks sizzling from the cord. Sylvie lay crumpled on the floor, her one hand blackened, her body eerily still.

"Call an ambulance," I shouted, dropping down next to my sister. "Someone go get my bag out of the car."

No breathing. No heartbeat. I saw the burns on her hand and realized this wasn't a burn from the fire beginning to consume our microwave or from the explosion. It was electrocution. Tears blurred my vision and I started CPR, trying to shove my emotions back until I had time to deal with them.

"Come on, Sylvie, come on," I chanted as I timed chest compressions. In the background, I heard Glenda on the phone and the slam of the door as someone ran for my medical bag. I heard Cassie's wail of fear and grief. Lucien stepped up and snapped his fingers, extinguishing the microwave fire before yanking the cord from the wall. He yelped as he touched it, shaking his hand. Good thing he was a demon, or I'd be trying to do CPR on two instead of one.

"Come *on*, Sylvie," I demanded, bending to breathe into her mouth.

A figure stepped up next to us. Even before I raised my head, I knew who it was. Babylon gasped, confirming my suspicions. I knew no one but me could see the reaper—well, no one but me and my necromancer sister.

"No, no, no!" Babylon shrieked, then burst into tears. "Go away. You can't have her! Go away."

"Who?" Magic sparked along Cassie's fingers as she scanned the room. "Who can't have her? Lonnie, who's here?"

"A reaper," Lucien said. He and Hadur were both looking right at the man. Evidently demons could see him as well as me and my youngest sister.

A reaper. Babylon had been right. I heard the sounds of the siren, felt my own pulse roaring through me as I counted out chest compressions. Sylvie couldn't die. She couldn't. She was my twin, half of my whole. Electrocuted by a damned microwave? She was a luck witch. How could this possibly happen to a luck witch?

I guess even luck witches weren't lucky forever.

No. It wasn't going to happen. I wasn't going to lose my sister. Looking up, I motioned for Bronwyn to take over and stood, ready to assist the paramedics coming through the door. That's when everything stopped.

I mean *stopped*. The paramedics were halfway through the kitchen door with bags and a stretcher. Bronwyn was doing artificial respiration. Babylon was mid-sob. The only two people who were moving in this weird frozen tableau were me and the reaper.

"A life for a life, my darling," he told me. "It's time for you to make a choice, and either way you choose, nothing will be the same."

A choice. Like on the mountaintop in my vision. I'd need to make a choice, and there was death down either path.

I caught my breath, realizing what he was saying, what the vision must have meant. The reaper was asking me to trade my life for my sister's. Either way, my family was going to lose somebody today—me or Sylvie. Call me a coward, but I didn't even hesitate. I couldn't live with the scenario where my twin died in my arms, where I was unable to save her. I only hoped that Sylvie was stronger than I was and that she'd recover from my loss.

"Yes. Save her. I'll do anything to save her. I'll trade my life for hers, I'll give my soul to the devil, I'll give up all my witch powers. Anything. I'll even let you have my car and every dime in my checking account. If you've been looking for a sweet Audi A4, then the keys are in my purse by the table. Take it and go. Take me and go. Just don't take my sister."

Something sparking to life in his dark eyes. "I'm a reaper. This is my purpose—to ease souls from their mortal forms and usher them into their afterlife. It's not my job to make the decisions in who lives or dies. I merely assist in the process."

I stepped forward, my decision made. "You said make a choice; well, I've made it. A life for a life. I'm good with that. Deal."

The pallor of his skin warmed. Not quite tan, but not quite so pale. The black eyes became more of a dark brown. "If she lives, she may live for another week, another year, or another three decades, but eventually she will die. You can never escape death, only delay it."

"Well, how about delaying it for another seventy years or so? How about she just not die today? Let her live." I stepped into him and reached up to touch his face. His skin was cool and dry, but not cold. "You've done it before. The goblin?

The man in the car accident two years ago? That gargoyle the other night? You say you have no control over life or death, but that's a lie. I've seen it. I've seen miracles occur, and I believe those miracles were because you willed them."

"It's one thing to delay and allow magic and medicine more time to save a life. This is different. I can't let this one go," he insisted, reaching up to take my hand in his. "This is different. If she lives, another dies."

"I told you that I'd trade my life for hers. That's my bargain." I told him. "I'll do anything for her. Anything. Just please, please don't let her die."

He inhaled, and I suddenly wondered if he'd been breathing before. Maybe reapers were like vampires and only had to breathe to talk? I didn't have long to ponder the question because he leaned down and kissed me.

I've been kissed before. I've been kissed a whole lot before. I've done a whole lot of things other than kissing in my life. But this was amazing. Heat shot through me and before I realized what was going on, I was pressed against him with my arms wrapped around his neck. When I came up for air, I was really regretting that I was about to be dead and I wouldn't get the chance to drag this guy off to bed like I wanted to.

My last kiss. It really sucked that I couldn't get more than that before my soul headed off to wherever. Purgatory? Heaven? Hell? I wondered if I went to hell if I could drop Lucien's name and hopefully get special treatment. I better. Cassie would never forgive him if he let his father's minions boil me in oil for all eternity.

Well, if I was going to die, then I was going to go for it. Time was stopped. I didn't need to feel guilty about doing this reaper while my sister lay dying because I'd just bargained away my life for hers. And it wasn't like any of my sisters or their demon mates could see me getting naked and busy with this guy—at least I didn't think so. And if they could? Oh, well, I was going to be dead anyway. I wouldn't be alive to endure Sylvie critiquing my technique, or Cassie teasing me about my pale ass. Condemned prisoners got a last meal. Well, I wanted a last screw.

I closed my eyes and leaned in to kiss him again, only to find myself standing in the kitchen with my arms stretched up in the air like a ballet dancer's. Sound roared back to life —the bustle and shouts of the paramedics, Babylon's sobs. In the midst of it all, I heard Bronwyn shout.

"She's breathing! I've got a pulse and she's breathing!"

I spun around to see Sylvie drag in a ragged breath, her eyes fluttering open. The paramedics pushed Bronwyn aside and knelt next to my twin, attaching monitors, an oxygen canula, and taking her vitals. I held back, wrapping my arms around myself as I watched. My sisters. I loved them all so much. Yes, Sylvie was my twin and we had a special bond, but every one of these women were as important to me as the very breath of life.

Was this the last time I'd see them? Would I just drop dead on the ground? Keel over as they carted Sylvie off to the hospital for observation? Would I even get a chance to say goodbye? Maybe it would be easier if I *didn't* say goodbye. Part of me wished it would just happen now. Get it over with before I started bawling my eyes out about how I might never see my sisters again.

Where was that reaper? What was his name again? Nash, or something? This would be a whole lot easier if he were here by my side. Or kissing me.

And, yeah...that kiss. Was that some reaper, soul-stealing thing? Was I already dead and didn't even know it?

"Oh, Ophelia!" Cassie came over and hugged me tight. "She's going to be okay. Don't look like that. She's fine. She'll be okay."

I slowly eased the breath from my lungs and tried to relax in my sister's arms. Guess I wasn't astral projecting, hovering over my dead body after all. When *was* I going to die? I'd just assumed it would be an instantaneous swap. Did I get a few extra hours to take care of things? Write a fast will? Let Cassie know where I'd stored my old spell books? Burn those journals from my teen years that I really didn't want anyone to read?

"I thought we were going to lose her." My voice wavered a bit. "I thought she was going to die."

Cassie gave me another bone-crushing hug. "Well, she's not. And I'm getting the damned electric fixed in this house. Completely rewired. I don't think it's been touched since 1950. Everything's probably rotted or mouse-chewed. She'll be fine, and I'll fix this so it won't ever happen again."

That was Cassie. She was always the take-charge sister, the fix-it-all one among us. I think it came from having to take care of six younger sisters when she was only thirteen. But I knew my eldest sister enough to hear what she wasn't saying. She blamed herself for this. It was her house. Yes, it was the family home we'd all grown up in, but she'd taken charge of it, assumed caretakership of it just as she'd done us. And in her mind, faulty wiring was a personal failing on her part.

"It was a freak accident," I assured her. "I've seen a few electrocutions in my time, and they've always been just a perfect storm of unfortunate circumstances all coming together at once. She's alive. She'll be okay, and that's all that matters."

Here I was reassuring my eldest sister that she wasn't to blame. Would she feel guilty when I paid the price and she found me dead? I hoped not, but knowing Cassie, she'd shoulder that responsibility as she'd always done.

Cassie let go of me and the pair of us walked over to

where they were loading Sylvie onto a stretcher. My twin looked up at me and her eyes met mine in a wordless exchange we'd been doing since we were still in the cradle.

"Mffr, mfrf mfrf," she said into the oxygen mask they'd slapped over her mouth. I guess they decided the canula wasn't as effective as they'd wanted.

"Can't understand you," I told her. "But if you're wondering about the hot fudge, I hate to tell you but it's a goner. In an incredible act of selfless sacrifice, the hot fudge took the brunt of the electrical surge, giving its life so that *you* might live another day."

It *was* pretty close to what had happened if one were to substitute hot fudge for me, but my joke did what I'd intended it to do. Sylvie started to laugh, fogging up the mask and earning me a stern glance from Flora, my Valkyrie co-worker.

They began to wheel Sylvie out with the rest of us trailing behind.

Cassie reached out to take my arm. "Do you want to ride in with her?"

She desperately wanted to do it, to be the one taking care of my sister and fussing over her as she'd fussed over all of us for most of our lives, but she was deferring to me as the twin. Cassie knew we had a bond that was a bit different than the rest of us had, and I appreciated that she would step aside and let me go to the hospital with Sylvie in her stead, but I had a date with a reaper and I really didn't want to drop dead right in front of my twin who was recovering from being electrocuted. Better to let Cassie take charge and do what she did best while I hopefully died peacefully somewhere in a way that wouldn't overly traumatize my sisters.

"You go," I told Cassie. "I'll stay here and clean up and take care of things, and I'll swing by the hospital afterward."

She gave me a quick kiss on the cheek, then turned to

Lucien, telling him that she'd call him when she needed him to come pick her up from the hospital. The demon, evidently either used to being ordered around or so incredibly besotted with my sister that he was blind to her bossy ways, agreed.

We watched as Flora and the others loaded Sylvie into the ambulance. Cassie climbed in beside them, her hand on my twin's shoulder. They closed the doors and drove off. We watched for a while after they'd turned the corner and vanished from view, as if we were thinking they might suddenly return. Then slowly we filed back inside where ice cream was melted to liquid in bowls on the dining room table, and the kitchen was a blackened mess of blasted microwave and exploded hot fudge. And with all the silent speed of a robot army set to slow, we all began to clean up.

CHAPTER 8

OPHELIA

*N*obody felt like eating ice cream, so it all went down the sink and in the trash. Glenda headed home to start work on some healing potions for Sylvie. Aaron and Adrienne hauled the microwave out back behind the house where the trash cans were, then began scrubbing the counter and floors while Bronwyn, Babylon, and I cleaned up the rest of the dinner. Hadur and Lucien went down in the basement to find a can of paint, then began covering up the scorch marks. We all wanted Cassie to return to a home that wasn't a glaring reminder that we'd almost lost a sister.

One by one we left, hugging each other with the poignant awareness that our bond was a precious one. I was still alive, so I decided to grab the leftover baked ziti from dinner and take it down to the guys and gals at the station as a bit of a thank you for rushing to our aid tonight.

As I went to leave, I found Lucien blocking my way.

"There was a reaper here tonight," he said. "Hadur and I saw him. Babylon saw him. You saw him."

There was no sense denying it at this point. "Yes. I've

actually seen him before—quite a few times before on ambulance runs. When I told Cassie about him, we'd figured he was a ghost or a freaky stalker who had a thing for accident scenes. I didn't know he was a reaper until I talked to Babylon about him."

"I don't know how much experience you've had with reapers, but they don't show up unless someone is dead or is going to die," Lucien told me.

"Well, clearly this reaper jumps the gun," I countered.

He frowned. "What do you mean?"

"Dead is such a subjective term," I told him. "A heart stopping. Someone not breathing. We've got drugs and technology and what used to be considered dead, no longer is actually dead. It's only at the point where there's no hope that their bodies will take on those essential functions again that a person is really dead."

"So, you're saying this guy has shown up at false calls before." Lucien eyed me skeptically. "Why don't they adjust for this sort of thing? Like wait a bit before appearing, just to make sure they're really needed."

"I know! It's terribly inefficient of them. Reapers clearly need to adjust their processes. Especially this guy. Just the other day, he showed up to a drowning and the goblin lived. Dude is gonna get fired if he doesn't stop wasting his time on people who aren't actually going to die."

I said a silent apology to the reaper in question, hoping he wasn't the sort who took offense. Lucien couldn't know what I'd done. If he found out, he'd tell Cassie because he told Cassie everything, then my sisters would all know including Sylvie. I didn't want her to feel guilty that I'd taken her place. I didn't want her to blame herself. My imminent death needed to seem unrelated to her near miss.

"I've never known a reaper to arrive and not be needed."

Lucien narrowed his eyes. "When I saw him there, I knew that Sylvie was going to die."

"Well, clearly you were wrong. You haven't been in the human world for long, and your last visit before this was what? Fifty years ago? A hundred years ago? Medicine has improved since then. I'm sure reapers go back empty handed a lot nowadays, and I'm also sure this guy screws up more than most."

Sylvie would be crushed if she knew I'd given my life for hers. I couldn't let anyone know. I had to somehow convince Lucien that this reaper had just made a mistake, and then when I dropped dead in a bowl of soup tomorrow afternoon, he wouldn't make the connection.

Who was I kidding? Of course he'd make the connection. One sister nearly dies but has a miraculous recovery, only for her twin to die less than twenty-four hours later? Lucien wasn't stupid. And neither were my sisters.

They were going to be so brokenhearted. But they would have been just as brokenhearted over losing Sylvie. There were no good choices in all this, just like in that stupid vision of mine.

"How well do you know that reaper?" Lucien's gaze bore into me, and I was suddenly reminded of the fact that he wasn't just my sister's adoring boyfriend. He was a demon. And not just any demon, either. He was the son of Satan.

"Like I told you, he's been showing up at my accident scenes for the last two years. He always hangs around, watching me. At least, I think he's watching me. Maybe he's watching the injured person instead. Either way, he vanishes by the time we get the patient into the ambulance and I don't see him again until the next call. And he doesn't come to all calls, just the very serious ones—the life or death ones. Most times he leaves empty handed, so it's not like what happened tonight is all that unusual for him."

"So, you don't know him that well."

Oh, for Pete's sake. "Well, I *did* ask him out to dinner, but he hasn't given me a yes or a no on that yet."

"Stop joking, Ophelia. This isn't funny."

"I'm not joking. I really did ask him out. Dinner, or maybe coffee if dinner is moving too fast. Do reapers eat? Maybe I should have just invited him over to Netflix and chill instead."

Lucien rolled his eyes. "Witches."

Yes, we were crazy, all seven of us.

"The thing that surprises me is that you can see this reaper. Have you seen other reapers in the past? Why only this one? And why you?"

"No, I haven't seen other reapers in the past. I have no idea why I only see this one. And it's not just me—Babylon can see him too," I replied, ticking the answers off on my fingers.

"Babylon is a necromancer and thus she's technically a spirit-worker. Although I wouldn't normally be surprised that an oracle can see a reaper, I wonder why you haven't seen one before. Why this one? Why now?"

"I don't know." I threw up my hand, the one not holding leftover baked ziti, in exasperation. "What are you getting at, Lucien? Maybe my sensitivity to them has increased as I've become older and grown more powerful. Maybe he switched territories with another reaper and I just happen to be able to see this particular one. Maybe the first time he saw me he fell desperately in love with me and that's why I can see him."

Why had he kissed me? Was that some seal-the-deal kiss? A I'm-taking-part-of-your-soul kiss? Or was it a kiss-kiss? I was really hoping it was a kiss-kiss.

"Okay." Lucien stepped aside but eyed me with a narrowed gaze. "But if you see him again, I want you to tell me. Or Cassie."

Good grief, they really were a pair. Both of them bossy as all get out.

"Fine. I'm going to swing by the hospital, then drop this off at the fire house, then go home. And I will definitely let you or Cassie know if I encounter any reapers along my way." I pushed past him and headed out the door, unreasonably angry.

No, not angry. I was flustered. I was scared. I'd almost lost one of my sisters, and I'd just bargained away my life. I was going to die. Maybe now, maybe tonight, maybe Monday, but I was going to die. And although I'd made the bargain in good faith, I'd be lying if I didn't admit that I was terrified.

I put the baked ziti in the trunk of my car, then went around to the driver's side, yelping in fright as I slid into the seat and saw someone sitting beside me. It was the reaper. And he seemed just as unnerved as I was.

"What the hell...?" I sputtered. "Is this it? Are my sisters going to find me dead in my car in front of Cassie's house? Because I think I just had a fatal heart attack here."

"Sorry. I wasn't sure where to go. I'm not sure what to do...what's going on. All I know is that I have to be near you." He stared at me a moment then looked down at his hands. That's when I realized that for the first time since I'd begun seeing him, he looked like a normal guy. I mean, he was just as hot, but he didn't have that ghostly reaper-ish pallor.

I sighed. "Of course you have to be near me. Just give me a head's up when it's my time, okay? And don't sneak around like this."

He glanced over at me, and his expression was so confused, so forlorn that I felt sorry for him. A reaper. There was a reaper sitting in my passenger seat following me around and waiting for my imminent death, and I had an urge to hug him and make him a cup of hot cocoa.

What had happened to cool, calm, collected, and confident? Was this the first time he'd done this sort of bargaining deal? A life for a life? Perhaps he had gotten a bit attached to me over the last few years and was bummed our little thing was coming to an end. Maybe he was regretting he hadn't taken me up on my dinner offer before I signed my life away.

Could I date a reaper if I were dead? Was there a diner or hibachi grill in the afterlife we could go to? The thought of never seeing him again made me just as depressed as the thought of my death.

"What was your name again?" I asked. "I've been calling you Nash because I couldn't remember."

"Nirnasha. But I would like for you to call me Nash."

I started the car. "Okay, Nash the reaper. If I'm not about to die in the next hour or so, here's my agenda. I'm going to the hospital to see my sister, then I'm going to swing by the fire station and drop off this baked ziti. Then if I'm still alive, I'm going home to catch some z's because today has just drained all the life out of me—pun intended."

He didn't reply. In fact, he remained silent the entire drive to the hospital. It made me a bit nervous to be driving around with a reaper in my passenger seat, and I couldn't think of anything to say to him, so I turned on some music. I'm kinda old school at heart, so I found a classic rock station which unfortunately was playing "Stairway to Heaven."

Grimacing, I turned the radio off and just resigned myself to drive in silence. Once at the hospital, Nash followed me inside. He waited patiently while I found out what room they'd admitted Sylvie to, then trailed after me down the halls and into the elevator.

"Stay here," I told him once we were outside Sylvie's room. "I don't know if Sylvie saw you while she was dead, and I don't want to freak her out. Either way, I don't want to answer a bunch of questions from Cassie about who you are and why I brought you with me to the hospital."

He hesitated and for a second, I thought he was going to argue, but then he meandered across the hall to a little sitting area, plopped into a chair, and picked up a magazine.

I went inside, a little worried about the wisdom of leaving a reaper unattended in the hospital. He'd said he didn't have power over life and death, but Sylvie had basically been resurrected, so I didn't have much faith in the truth of that theory. What if I came out of Sylvie's room to find that he'd reaped the souls of everyone in the hospital? A mass casualty event, and it would be all my fault because I had a reaper following me around. Maybe I should have just insisted that I die in Cassie's driveway.

Once inside the room, I put all thoughts of Nash from my mind and concentrated on Sylvie who was looking…well, like she'd had a near-death experience.

"Gorgeous, huh?" She smiled weakly at me. Dark circles tinted the skin under her eyes, and she seemed thinner and paler than before. One of her hands was bandaged—the one that had been burned.

"Yes, you do look gorgeous." I crossed the room and kissed her cheek. "Where's Cassie?"

Sylvie shot me an impish smile. "I sent her down to get me ice cream. I didn't get to have mine at the house."

"None of us got to have any."

Her smile faltered. "That's my fault."

I sat down in the chair and put my hand on her shoulder. "No, it's not. It's an old house. The wiring was bad. We're all just thankful that you're okay."

"Or that the house didn't burn down." She forced a laugh. "I'm a luck witch, Ophelia. This isn't supposed to happen to me."

"It's probably a good thing it *did* happen to you. Luck witch means you're still alive. If it had been Glenda or Adrienne or any of us who'd gone to microwave the hot fudge, we might not have made it."

That was my story, and I was going with it. There was no sense in having everyone wonder about why Sylvie had been basically dead and survived, no sense in having my family connect my soon-to-be-death with Sylvie's resurrection. It was better to just say she'd been lucky. And of course she *had* been lucky. It was her gift.

"How are you feeling?" I asked.

"Like I was electrocuted." Her smile wavered and fell. "I think I was dead, Ophelia. I don't want to say anything to Cassie or the others. I don't want to freak them out, but I think I was dead. You're my twin. We've always had this thing between us. What happened when I was laying there on the kitchen floor? What really happened?"

I gave her shoulder a reassuring squeeze. "Your heart stopped. You weren't breathing. We called 911 and I did CPR, then Bronwyn took over for a little bit. By the time the paramedics got there, you were back with us. You were lucky."

"I was dead," she insisted.

"Lots of people have had near-death experiences, Sylvie. That's what happened."

She frowned, considering my words. "This felt different. This felt dead-dead. But maybe you're right. I've never had this happen before, so I don't know what a near-death experience feels like."

"Hovering above your body? A long tunnel with light at the end?" I suggested. "I think that's what other people have said they experienced."

She nodded. "Someone was there, and it was like they were there to cut the cord or something, but they hesitated. I waited and waited and began to wonder what was going on, then *whoosh*. I was gasping for air and everything felt like I'd been run over by a truck."

I skated my hand down her arm to hold her non-burned hand. "I'm glad he didn't cut the cord. I'm glad you came back to us."

Her eyes searched mine. "What did you do, Ophelia? You're not telling me something. What did you do?"

Before I could open my mouth to lie, Cassie came back in the room carrying a little dish of soft-serve vanilla. By her side was Glenda, and *she* was carrying a thermos.

I knew what was in that thermos. Glenda was the only one of us that healed, and she performed her magic by creating the most horrible-tasting organic smoothies in the world. How such an amazing chef couldn't manage to make her magical elixirs more palatable was beyond me. Honestly, I think that having the flu or a broken leg would be preferable to downing that heinous concoction.

"Here's your ice cream," Cassie announced.

"And here's your medicine." Glenda unscrewed the cap and picked up a plastic cup from a bedside table, pouring a disgusting thick green substance into the cup. It smelled like herrings and seaweed.

"I don't think I need that," Sylvie announced, wrinkling her nose.

"Nonsense. Of course you need this. Muscle, nerve, and tissue damage are frequently long-term effects of electrocution."

Sylvie looked up at me and I nodded. "She's right. Drink the fishy seaweed smoothie, then wash it down with your ice cream."

My twin took a deep breath, picked up the cup, and threw down the drink with the speed of a werewolf shooting cheap whisky in a bar. Then she slammed the cup on the table and shuddered, screwing up her face and sticking out her tongue.

"Every two hours until it's gone," Glenda announced cheerfully as she sat the thermos on the table next to the empty cup.

"You outdid yourself, Glenda," Sylvie told her. "That was the most horrible thing I've ever tasted in my whole life."

I'm sure it was horrible, but Sylvie would drink it partly because Glenda was a talented witch and her magic did what no doctor could do, and partly because if she threw it out or refused it, Glenda's feelings would be hurt. None of us wanted that.

I leaned down to kiss my twin on the cheek, scooting the ice cream over closer to her. "I'm going to head out. I'll swing by tomorrow and see you. I can give you a ride home if they release you."

"No, I'm doing that," Cassie announced. "I'm spending the night here, and I'll have Lucien come over and pick us up after they let her out. Sylvie is going to stay at my house until she's *completely* recovered."

Sylvie and I exchanged a knowing glance. This was Cassie. Bossy. Overprotective. She'd assumed a maternal role when our mother lit out, and even now that we were all grown, she still felt one hundred percent responsible for us. It was something we put up with because we loved her—just like we put up with Glenda's disgusting smoothies.

I left Sylvie's room, and I found Nash over by the nurses' station, flirting.

At least, I think he was flirting. The nurses certainly thought so and that made me feel a bit stabby. Evidently flirting, according to some weird reaper social conventions, involved asking the nurses about their jobs as well as what various monitors and medications were, and having them demonstrate. When I walked up, he had a blood pressure cuff on, and an attractive blonde was standing close enough that her boobs were touching his arm as she read the results.

I leaned over as well, wondering what sort of cardiac function a reaper had. It was disappointingly normal.

"Are you coming with me, or shall I leave you here at the hospital?" Although leaving a reaper at a hospital probably wasn't a good idea. Hopefully no one had died while I was in talking to Sylvie.

"Thank you for the demonstration." He took the cuff off and handed it to the blonde whose boobs were still practically glued to his arm.

"Come back later and I'll show you how the dialysis machine works. I'm here until tomorrow noon."

"Trust me, you don't want him to come back here," I told her as I grabbed Nash's arm and pulled him away. I kept a tight grip on him as we waited for the elevator, worried he would run back to the blonde if I let him go.

I should have let him stay with the nurse. Maybe he would have forgotten about me and our bargain if he went back to her. It *really* wasn't jealousy over the nurse that kept my hand on his arm; it was that I didn't want to endanger any of the patients here by having a reaper present. Yeah, that was it.

"Please tell me you didn't kill anyone while I was in with Sylvie." We boarded the elevator and I pushed the ground floor button with one hand, still holding onto him with the other.

"I don't *kill* people. I ease their souls from their body so they can journey to their afterlife."

"Tomato, tomahto. That sounds like killing to me."

"There's a difference," he insisted.

"*How* is there a difference?" We got out of the elevator I was still holding his arm as we walked across the lobby. He waited to respond until we were in the parking lot, and I wasn't sure if that was because he didn't want anyone to hear or because he needed to seriously think about the question.

"I sever the cord. I release the soul which has already separated. I facilitate, but I don't initiate."

I spun around to face him, realizing that I was just as close to him as the blonde had been.

"What happens when you don't cut the cord? Is that when people miraculously live? You refusing to do your job means someone doesn't die, right?"

He looked down at me with that cool, confident expression he'd always had over the two years I'd been seeing him, but behind it all was confusion, as if he were out of his element and in completely new territory.

"I'll admit there have been times when I've delayed, and that delay has allowed human intervention to work its magic."

"Is that what happened with Sylvie?"

"No." He looked down at my hand on his arm, then back up at me. "She was resurrected. Her soul had fully separated, and I refused to cut the final strand. I didn't reap her soul. I returned it to her mortal form. I gave her new life. And what I did is forbidden."

Forbidden? "But as long as you take another life, it's all good, right? You said a life for a life, so Sylvie gets resurrected, and it's all good as long as someone else dies?"

"The scales must balance," he told me, sounding more like a reaper and less like a mortal in that moment.

It scared me. Sometimes he seemed human, and sometimes like this, he seemed otherworldly. And when he was a reaper, he was more terrifying than the demons, more frightening than a banshee's howl.

I cleared my throat, wanting to forget about my looming death and discuss something else instead. "Tell me about your reaperness, or job, or whatever it is. Do you guys have pagers? How do you know where to go and who to go to? Do you clock in and get your assignments each day, or what?"

His eyes lightened just a shade. "It just happens. We go where we're needed then we wait for the right moment and release the soul from its body. Normally, we don't determine where we go and when, or who we come for. We get the order and we go."

"Normally?"

He reached out and touched my cheek. "Two years ago, I came to reap a soul and saw you. Something changed and ever since then, I've been the only reaper to come here. It's as if I'm bound to this area...bound to you."

"Me?" I squeaked, torn between alarm that one of death's minions had attached himself to me and flattery that he'd chosen me out of seven billion humans to stalk. It was so romantic. We were brought together by a near-death experience two years ago, bound tight by the opposing nature of our job duties, only to be separated by my death before we even had a chance to share a candlelit dinner and a romantic moonlight stroll.

Okay, maybe that was tragedy instead of romance.

"You." His thumb stroked my cheek. "You've made a choice, a decision, and there's no turning back now."

My decision. My choice. Death down either path. I wondered when the rest of my vision would come into play —the blood on the oleanders, the smell of decay at the edge of a woods...golf balls. I guess it all meant I was going to die in a park somewhere, or on a golf course, taken out by a stray ball. Figures that the only time I unraveled the meaning of a death prediction, it was my own.

"No, there's no turning back," I whispered, trying to steel myself for what was to come.

His hand slid along my jaw, fingers brushing my lips. "We reapers are not...we're not human. We're not angels, nor are we demons. We exist to perform a specific function and that's all we do."

This...this was weird, because I was getting super turned on all while wondering if I was going to die in this parking lot right now. Was there an oleander bush nearby? Someone golfing?

His eyes searched mine. "Until I first saw you, my life was devoid of emotion, of anything but my purpose. But the moment I was in your presence, I knew happiness and pain, life and death."

It was the most romantic thing anyone had ever said to me. Weird and kinda creepy, but romantic.

"You've been holding off reaping souls for *me*?" I waited for his nod. "You've been allowing me and my co-workers time to bring someone back, because of *me*? That man in the car accident two years ago? The gargoyle the other night? The goblin? The coyote shifter? The sylph last summer? The gnome with that tunnel cave-in? The vampire with the tanning bed?"

He smiled, and I got the impression it was the first time that he'd ever done so. "And the satyr."

"The one with his...you know, stuck in the industrial-strength vacuum cleaner?" I asked. "The one who nearly bled to death trying to remove himself?"

He nodded.

"They all lived because...because you have a thing for me."

"I delayed. I did not reap a soul until there was absolutely no possibility that the body would survive. And yes, I did this because of you."

"Two years. All those touch-and-go cases for two years, all the ones that miraculously lived, that was because of me?"

His hand moved down and around under my hair to cup the back of my neck. "I couldn't help myself, even though each time I died just a little. I saw how distraught you were, how much you wanted those people to live, and I found myself unable to take their souls."

I felt the sting of tears. He'd done this for me. No one had ever cared about me this much besides my sisters. He'd let people live just because I wanted them to live. But what price had he paid for doing that? Was that why I'd had to trade my life for Sylvie's? Was he one soul away from some sort of eternal punishment or oblivion? He'd said what he had done was forbidden. What would become of him once he'd taken my soul and sent me off to the afterlife? Would he go back to that cold emotionless existence he'd had before, where the only thing that happened was reaping souls? Maybe we were *both* doomed for tragedy.

"I'm sorry," I whispered, meaning that apology to encompass everything. "I'm so sorry."

Then I stood on my tip-toes and kissed him. It was a soft, butterfly-light kiss, but something happened the moment my lips touched his. His hand tightened on the back of my neck, his other arm reaching around my waist to pull me closer. Fire roared up through me and before I knew it, I was pressed against the side of my car, yanking his shirt up as he kissed the holy hell out of me. My hands moved up the warm skin of his sides and I lifted one of my legs, curling it around behind him to grind myself against him.

"Hey!"

A spotlight shone on us and we froze.

"Knock it off, guys. This is a hospital. The maternity ward's over there. Maybe you should make your way to that section, just in case."

Ha, ha, very funny. I peered over Nash's shoulder and blinked at the bright light.

"Ophelia? Is that you?" The man laughed and I realized, much to my embarrassment, that I knew him. Of course I knew him. This was Accident and I knew pretty much everyone in town. I especially knew the staff here at the hospital including the security people.

Nash moved to the side, keeping one arm around my waist. The beam from the flashlight lowered and I could see the Fetch in front of us. Fetch were doppelgangers, but here in Accident, we had rules that limited them to three distinct forms since that was the only way we could keep track of them.

"Hey, Daniel."

The Fetch laughed again then flicked off the flashlight and ran a hand over his bald head. His eyes glowed bright green in the dimly lit parking lot. "Well then, you kids have a good evening. Use condoms. And get a room unless you don't care about half the town seeing you getting porked in the hospital parking lot, Ophelia."

He wandered off, whistling to himself and Nash turned to me with that puzzled, very human, expression on his face once more.

"Ophelia? What are condoms?"

CHAPTER 9

OPHELIA

"Whoa! Is that what I think it is?" Skip walked up and took the dish of baked ziti from my hands, then bent down to give me a quick kiss on the top of my head. He had to bend way down because Skip was a giant. Thankfully he was on the small side as giants go and only ten foot six inches, but that was still way taller than my five foot seven.

Flora poked her head out of the back room. "Did you bring us leftover pasta? Ophelia, you're the best."

I smiled as the Valkyrie walked toward me. "It's the least I could do for you guys taking care of my sister."

"Girl, you did all the hard work. We just drove her to the hospital." Flora took the dish from Skip and inhaled. "Shall I warm this up? It's got to be better than those tofu burgers Pierre tried to feed us earlier."

I wrinkled my nose. We all took turns cooking when we were on shift, and this was Pierre's week. Vampires suck at cooking. Although it's not like Pierre could eat anything he made, or that we made when it was our turn to cook. Blood was the only thing on the menu for him.

"Who's the hottie?" Flora's silver eyes roamed over Nash, and she twitched her dark wings in appreciation.

"This is Nash," I told them. "He's a reaper."

Skip chuckled. "Hope he's not here for any of us."

"No, although I'm sure I'll be seeing you all soon," Nash replied.

I grimaced. "Okay, well, let's not talk about our eventual deaths, shall we? Nash, this is Flora, who is an emergency medical technician along with the aforementioned Pierre and Ricky. Skip is a firefighter, as is Edward and Brandy."

"Edward, Ricky, and Brandy are off today," Skip chimed in.

"I work Thursday, Friday, and Saturday," I told Nash. "Thirteen-hour shifts. Sometimes Sundays depending on who else is working. We've got volunteers as well to help fill in the gaps."

"Which is important when one of your EMTs is a vampire," Flora drawled. "Sunlight and all that stuff. Edward mostly works nights as well. Gargoyles aren't exactly on their A-game during the day."

"Are there a lot of fires in your town?" Nash looked around at the equipment and the ladder truck.

Skip laughed. "Uh, let's see. Dragons. Chimera. Ifrits. Oh, and Ophelia's oldest sister. Yeah, I think fire is a bit of a problem."

"Actually, there are more medical calls than fire ones," Flora said. "You mix this many supernatural creatures together in one town, and you're going to end up with all sorts of weird medical emergencies. Luckily most of our town residents have exceptional healing skills."

But some didn't. I thought of that female gargoyle a few days ago, and the goblin who'd nearly drowned and shivered. Nash reached out and put an arm around my shoulder, giving it a quick squeeze and a smile.

"Are you okay?" he asked.

Oddly enough, I was. My sister had nearly died. I'd traded my life for hers and was expecting to drop dead at any minute. The reaper who'd resurrected my sister was probably facing some horrible fate for intervening. But Nash's arm around my shoulder, the calm confident smile he'd sent my way—it made me feel a zing of happiness. I got the feeling everything would be all right. Having an agent of death right next to me, touching me, sent all those fears I'd had since childhood right out the window.

"So, Nash, as long as you don't intend on reaping any of our souls, why don't you join us in the break room for coffee? Pierre is making dessert, and as crappy as he is at making dinner, the vampire can manage to not ruin ready-to-bake cookies."

Nash sent a questioning glance my way and I nodded. "Sure. I'd like that."

Pierre was pulling cookies out of the oven as we walked in. Chocolate chip. Flora shoved the dish of baked ziti in place of the cookie tray and poured us all coffee as I introduced Nash to the vampire. Then we all sat down, drank coffee, and ate cookies while we talked about various calls we'd been on, whether Pistol Pete's was going to get a decent country and western band in for next weekend, and if the fairies planned to have their annual midsummer party or not. My co-workers were completely relaxed around Nash, welcoming him into the fold and teasing him mercilessly about how the pair of us met "on the job."

They thought he was my boyfriend. And none of them seemed bothered at all at the thought that I was dating a reaper. I guess in a town with trolls, and werewolves, and minotaur, and goblins, where the first responder crew was a witch, a gargoyle, a Valkyrie, a vampire, a sylph, a giant, and a bear shifter, someone dating a reaper wasn't a big deal.

Was he my boyfriend? It certainly seemed that way with his hand occasionally holding mine, his arm sometimes draped across my shoulder. We sat so close our shoulders and legs touched, and our gazes did linger when we looked at each other. He'd never said yes or no to my dinner invitation, but he'd met my co-workers, who seemed to love him. He'd resurrected my sister. And he'd kissed me. Twice.

Everything tingled at the remembrance of those kisses. Maybe I didn't have to die right away, and we could have some time together.

It was late when we headed back to my house. Both of us were silent during the trip, but I couldn't help reaching out to hold his hand as I drove. Never once did I think to take him to Hollister's Inn to stay. I just waited for him to get in the passenger seat of my car and took him to my house. It seemed right. It *felt* right.

Where the heck should he sleep? My bed? My pulse raced at the thought. I'd just met him. I should probably fix up the couch for him and take things slow, but I didn't want to take things slow. What if we didn't have time? What if tonight was all we had?

Once home, Nash followed me inside. I turned on the lights, tossed my keys on the counter, and turned to face him. "We need to talk. When am I going to bite the big one? Because I need to know how long I have. A day? A week? Do we have time for dinner and a movie? Do we have time for sex? Please tell me we have time for sex? I like you. I *really* like you. And normally I don't like to rush things like this, but if I'm going to keel over in my cereal tomorrow morning, then I kinda want to get busy tonight, if you know what I mean. So just lay it on the line. Tell it to me straight. When am I going to die?"

He blinked. "How would I know when you're going to die? You're the oracle, not me. I show up and reap a soul. It's not like I can predict when someone's going to die or not. That's not in my job description."

"So, you're just going to stay with me until it happens?"

"I don't know where else I'm supposed to go. Don't you want me here?" He sounded a bit hurt. "I don't want to impose. I guess it was rather presumptuous of me, but I want to be near you. I can leave."

"Don't leave. I *do* want you to stay here."

I liked him. He was hot, and I really wanted him in my bed, but there was more to it than that. Everything felt right with him around—which was pretty twisted, given what his job description entailed.

"Just promise me that it will be somewhere decent," I told him. "Not when I'm on the toilet, or while I'm driving and could hit someone. Not while I'm at work because that's not a good time, either. Maybe in my sleep? With my hair done and my makeup on and a nice pair of undies and some silky pajamas?"

Crap, I didn't own any silky pajamas. I really didn't want to be found dead in a threadbare Hard Rock Café shirt or a stained tank top. Maybe Nash could stall this whole reaping thing until I had time to run over the mountains to the mall and get a pretty lacy negligée at Victoria's Secret. Nothing too sleazy, though, because I didn't want my sisters to see me in some crotchless, nipple-baring number.

Nash stared at me and slowly shook his head. "What are you talking about?"

"My death." I blew out a breath in exasperation. "We made a deal. You said a life for a life, and I agreed to it. Sylvie lives and I die. But when? I can't keep walking around not knowing if it's going to be today or tomorrow or next week, my death hanging over my head like that sword of Damocles thing. Give me some idea of when. And then let's go screw, because that's on the top of my bucket list if you haven't real-ized it yet."

He squinted at me and slowly shook his head. "I don't know when you're going to die. That wasn't the deal."

"Then what *was* the deal?" I was tired. I was horny. I was drained emotionally. And I was scared that I was going to die before I got a chance to have sex with this reaper. "You said a life for a life."

"Yes. A life for a life. I'm a reaper. My job is to free souls from their mortal bodies. It's one thing to delay that and let mortal medicine have a chance to change the outcome. It's another to refuse to collect a soul. I refused to collect a soul, I *resurrected* someone, and there's a price that must be paid when that happens—a steep price."

"I know. I agreed to pay that price. I just want to know when it's going to happen as well as some assurance that I'll have clean underwear on at the time."

He stepped closer to me. "*You* don't pay that price. *I* do. I'm the one who refused to do my duty. I'm the one who resurrected a mortal. I'm the one who pays."

I caught my breath. "But you said a life for a life."

He nodded. "*My* life."

No. No, no, no. How could this happen? "That's not what I agreed to. I agreed to exchange my life for Sylvie's. It's not... you can't. I can't let you do this. That's not fair. I know you said you were going to be in trouble, but I thought my death would somehow even the score. I would have never agreed to this if I'd known *you* were the one who was going to die."

He gave me a sad smile. "It's too late to change things now. I offered. When I said, 'a life for a life,' I was letting you know what the ramifications would be."

"Why would you do this?" I shook my head in astonish-ment. "You don't know Sylvie. Why would you do this?"

"Because of you. I did this for you, Ophelia, because your

family is your life. When I saw you two years ago, everything changed. I cannot imagine existing without you. I would do anything for you. I know you feel the same about your sisters. I don't want to see you unhappy, so I laid down my scythe and refused to do what my sole purpose of existing is. I refused to reap, I resurrected a mortal, and I now I have paid the price. I'd do it again if I could. I'd do anything for you, anything to make you happy."

No. This was even worse than thinking I was the one who was going to die. He'd sacrificed himself for my sister because he…kind of loved me? My chest felt as if someone had put a truckload of boulders on it. I liked him. I really liked him. I got the feeling that with time, I might actually grow to love him.

It was a tragedy. A choice where both paths ended in death.

"How long do you have? Do you know?" I asked him.

His eyes searched mine. "It's already done. It was done the moment your sister took that breath on the kitchen floor."

"Done?" I walked over and put a hand on his chest. "So, you're dead. Like a zombie? Like one of Babylon's raised-from-the-dead animals?"

He put his hand over mine. "The life I had is gone. I have no idea what is going to happen, but I feel different. I'm still here. I'm stuck on this plane of existence with the mortals. I'm no longer a reaper. I gave up my life as a reaper—I died—for your sister to live."

"So, you're mortal, right? Just a normal human? You're not going to die tonight or tomorrow or anything because of what you did? The price you paid was to give up your reaper-ness and immortality, not give up life itself."

"I don't know. This has never happened to a reaper before. I honestly don't know if I'm a human or something else. I don't know if I'm mortal or not. All I know is I'm here and even if I wanted to leave, I can't. I no longer hear the call to go reap a soul. The rest...well, I guess I'll figure out the rest as I go."

"So you're basically fired?"

How crappy was that? One refusal to reap, one resurrection, and he was out of a job. No warning. No performance improvement plan. One strike and he was out. I wondered if reapers could collect unemployment?

One thing that was clear—I owed this man big time. He'd saved my sister's life. Actually, he'd brought her back from the dead. No matter what happened, he was staying here, on my dime, until we figured out who and what he was now and managed to get him a new job.

And then if he wanted to continue living in my house... well, I was getting the feeling I'd be absolutely thrilled about that. As long as he did his share of the chores, didn't use up all the hot water, put the toilet seat down when he was done peeing, and wasn't one of those guys who hogged all the covers.

"I'm sorry." He took a step back and my hand slid from his chest. "I'll leave. This really isn't fair to you. I agreed to die in your sister's place. I brought her back to life. That doesn't mean you owe me anything. It was my choice."

"No, it was *my* choice," I countered. "And I'd be a pretty crappy person if I let you starve and sleep on the street after you got fired for resurrecting my sister. You're staying here."

"Just for the night." He looked around. "I'll sleep on your couch. And tomorrow I'll figure something out."

I walked forward, grabbed him by the shirt, hauled him down to me, and kissed him. "*We'll* figure something out. Together. However long it takes, we'll do it together. And as for the couch..." I looked over at the piece of furniture. I wasn't going to die. He wasn't going to die. The poor guy had only been fired a few hours ago. Maybe I should take things slow and not totally jump his bones the first day he'd become an ex-reaper.

"Couch," he said in a firm tone of voice. Then he kissed me and let me tell you, that kiss was full of a whole lot of promise. "Couch tonight. Then once we figure things out, maybe I'll move to the bed if you're interested."

Wow, was I interested. "Can I join you on the couch? Is that against the rules?"

He bent down to kiss me again, but before his lips met mine, I heard a rumble that felt like it shook the foundations of my house.

We both looked down at Nash's stomach, which repeated the protest. I guess coffee and cookies in the firehouse weren't enough to fill him up. That's when it hit me.

"You've never eaten before! Pierre's ready-to-bake chocolate chip cookies and a cup of Folger's half-caf were the first food and drink you've ever had since getting fired from your reaper job?" I was horrified. His first meal should have been something incredible. And there wasn't much I could do to rectify the situation, either. I tended to eat out, and I doubted there was more than eggs, cheese, and a jar of pickles in my fridge.

"Can you stop saying I was fired?" he complained. "It makes me sound like I was a lousy reaper."

I raised my eyebrows, because he kind of *was* a lousy reaper, at least in the last two years. How many times had he delayed and given me the chance to save someone?

He sighed. "Okay. Fired. I just hate how that sounds, though."

"No, you're right," I told him. "Plus, we have to think about future job opportunities. Let's call it an unlawful termination. That will look so much better on a resume."

His stomach growled again. I grabbed his hand and led him over to the sofa. "Here. Sit. I'm going to get you some food, and we'll talk about how to sum up your prior experience. What skillset goes into being a reaper, and how could that translate into a future career?"

I headed to the fridge and started pulling out cheese and a summer sausage I'd bought Friday. Then I grabbed the jar of pickles, thinking we might as well finish them off.

"Punctuality?" Nash paced the floor instead of sitting on the sofa. "Although I doubt I could have been late if I wanted to. We just show up, you know."

"No one needs to know that," I told him. "People fluff their resumes all the time. Punctuality. What else? How about attention to detail?"

He snorted. "Except for the last two years when I've been too distracted by a sexy witch to actually perform my job duties in a timely fashion?"

I felt myself flush. Sexy witch? I liked that.

"Loyalty? You've been doing the same job without fail for, what? A couple thousand years?"

He kept pacing. "Yep. I'm so loyal I broke every rule and resurrected someone."

I walked over and put the food down on the coffee table, sitting on the sofa as he continued to wear a groove in my carpet. "Do you have any idea what you might want to do now that you're not a reaper? Butcher? Baker? Candlestick maker?"

"I don't know how to do any of those things. I don't know how to do anything except reap." He stopped pacing, his expression agitated. Reaching out a hand, he brushed his fingers along the leaves of a plant on my bookshelf. Right before my eyes, the leaves turned brown and dropped off, the stems of the plant shriveling and crumbling to the soil in the pot.

I jumped to my feet. "Did you just kill my basil? You just killed my basil plant, didn't you?"

"No, I didn't!" Nash shoved his hands behind his back, looking like he'd just gotten nabbed with his fingers in the cookie jar. It's all I could do to keep from laughing.

"You did too. Look at it. You touched my basil plant, and now it's dead. You killed it."

He looked over at the plant and frowned. "I'm sorry. If it's any consolation, I didn't actually kill it. Reapers don't kill."

I was totally holding back laughter. "You reaped my basil plant's soul?"

He shot me a wary look. "Not really. I mean, plants don't have souls like other beings do, and they don't require the assistance of reapers to transition."

"So, what exactly did you do to my plant? Because it was alive two seconds ago, and now it's dead."

"I uh…I just hurried things along a bit. Sped it up, but not by much."

"So, you're saying the plant was dying anyway?"

He nodded.

I couldn't hide my grin any longer. "So, you're saying that *I* was killing my basil plant, and *you* put it out of its misery?"

He tilted his head as he regarded me, a tiny smile at the corner of his mouth. "Can I suggest you not attempt to keep houseplants in the future?"

Now I laughed. And when I was done laughing, I threw a pillow at him.

He caught the pillow and walked over to sit on the sofa. "You're not angry? I know death upsets you. I was worried you would be angry."

I sat down beside him. "No, I'm not angry. I'm sad at my inability to keep a basil plant alive, but I don't get as upset over plant deaths as I do humans or other sentient beings." I took the pillow from him and curled it up in my arms. "But how did you do it? I thought you couldn't reap anymore? Maybe it wasn't technically reaping a soul, but what you did

87

to the basil plant isn't something a normal human should be able to do."

He scooted over closer to me. "I don't know. It just happened. I didn't even think about it. I could tell the plant was dying, and when I touched it, it just died."

"But you're fired. You're not supposed to be able to do that," I countered.

He shrugged. "I didn't think I could. I can't hear the call. I'm not being sent to reap other souls, but perhaps I still have the ability. I don't know if it's just plants, though. If a were-wolf or a human were to be dying, I don't know if I'd be able to reap their soul or not."

I hugged the pillow and thought. Maybe if he went on some calls with me at the firehouse, we could see what happened. If someone died and another reaper showed up, perhaps they'd let Nash have a go at it first just to see if he still could do the job.

Although I didn't know what good that skill was in the outside world. A freelance reaper? He'd be better off becoming a cable installation technician or something.

"Why does it bother you so? Death, I mean," he asked. "It's a transition. All of life is a transition. To live is to experience constant change. Death is just a part of that change."

"I don't want things to change. I like having oatmeal every morning, doing laundry on Wednesdays, meeting Sylvie for lunch Thursday afternoons, and having dinner with my family Sunday nights."

I wasn't a total whackadoodle, but I did like my routine. Sylvie said it was a reaction to Grandma dying and Mom taking off. Those two things had hit us one right after the other and rocked our world. I'd seen how it had affected my sisters, especially Cassie, and to cope with the grief and the fear, I'd done two things. I'd found comfort in a life full of routine, and I'd honed my divination skills to provide me with as few surprises as possible. Not that the latter always worked. My glimpses into the future were sometimes a jumbled mess of nonsense, and often they had nothing to do with what I truly wanted to see. Finding things, finding people, and weather prediction were my jam. I was also pretty accurate at my cupid-radar. Other than that, my accuracy was equal to that of a blind man trying to pin a tail on a donkey.

"What about good changes?" he asked.

I opened my mouth to tell him there were no such things as good changes only to realize I was wrong. Lucien coming into Cassie's life was a wonderful change. As was Hadur coming into Bronwyn's life. I was so happy for both of my sisters. Yes, the two demons changed our family dynamics quite a bit, and I'll admit it took some getting used to having them at Sunday dinner and as part of the family, but I adapted.

And Nash...I'd been terrified over losing Sylvie just as I'd been terrified when Bronwyn had her accident, but despite the disruption to my routine, I enjoyed having Nash here in my house, sitting beside me on my couch.

I only wish that he hadn't given up everything to be here with me. What would he do with himself if he could no longer be a reaper? What would give his new life meaning and purpose? He seemed content to be here with me, but what if that didn't last? He'd surely want more than just following me around all day.

"You reaped the plant," I pointed out. "Maybe you're still a reaper or a partial reaper. A semi-reaper. Maybe they didn't fire you but just put you on administrative leave? Suspension for a few years as a disciplinary action?"

He shook his head. "I no longer hear the call. Over a hundred thousand people die each day. We reapers are busy. If I were still a reaper, I would have been called to duty by now. I would have been called to release twenty to thirty souls in the last hour. But instead I've heard nothing."

Over a hundred thousand people a day. I had to fend off a panic attack at the thought. "How many reapers are there?"

"Three hundred."

Three hundred reapers. Now two hundred ninety-nine reapers. Would they replace Nash? Post a job opening some-where for qualified individuals to apply? Or did reapers just spring from the ether? They didn't seem to be angels, nor did they seem to be demons. What were they?

"The demons saw you in the kitchen when Sylvie had died," I said. "They knew you were a reaper. So, I take it you're not a demon?"

"No." He smiled. "We are not demons nor angels, although we have more in common with angels then those from the infernal realms. We're neutral. We obey neither heaven nor hell. We simply exist to ensure what is born dies and what dies is born."

"That's very existential of you." I pointed to my plant. "Returning to my original question—you seem to still have some of your reaper powers. Why is that?"

"I don't know."

And we were back to that again. I yawned, realizing it was way past my bedtime and it had been a stressful day. Getting up, I went over to the hall closet and pulled out some sheets and a blanket.

"Here. Eat some food. Sleep. Or watch television if you like. Do you know how to use the remote?"

He picked it up. "I'll figure it out."

I watched him turn on the television and hesitated for a few seconds before heading into my bedroom.

It had been a long time since I'd cuddled up against a man —just as long since I'd done more than cuddle up against a man. The last boyfriend I'd had was a merman which had worked out about as well as expected. Merfolk were always uncomfortable out of water for longer than a few hours at a time, and I got pruney with an extended soak. Plus, I didn't have his tolerance for cold water the way he did, and we were faced with an increasingly limited time together as the weather grew cold. The brief relationship didn't last past mid-September. Last time I saw him, he was happily embroiled in a ménage with a pair of nymphs while I'd gone on to have a lovely liaison with a few pints of ice cream and a week of Netflix streaming while on my couch.

Then there had been that one-night stand with one of the vampires, but both of us knew *that* wasn't going anywhere. Any guy more interested in my blood than my garden of love was no guy for me.

The human boyfriends hadn't worked out that well either.

Hopefully Nash would. And hopefully this Nash-on-the-couch thing would only be for one night.

I brushed my teeth, brushed my hair, washed all the essential parts to make sure my nether regions were squeaky clean and smelled of mountain spring breeze or something like that, just in case Nash got lonely and found his way into my bed. There wasn't much to choose from in terms of nightwear. My threadbare Hard Rock Café shirt was my go-to when heading off to bed, but it was far from sexy, especially with the mystery stain that was centered on my right boob when I put it on. I did have a sexy negligée, but the last time I'd worn it had been when I was dating Bron, the merman, and it seemed wrong to recycle it for use with another man. I finally settled on a fairly new pair of under-wear and a snug tank top with a little lace around the neckline. Then I touched up my makeup because I'd rather smear foundation and mascara all over my pillow than be bare-faced—well, at least for the first week or so. After that, it would be messy hair, my Hard Rock Café shirt, and my washed-out, pale-as-the-dead complexion. As a final touch, I rubbed a bit of cologne that had come in a magazine about four years ago on my cleavage and headed into the bedroom.

I could hear the television right outside my door. As a sort of last-ditch effort to lure the reaper into my bed, I sashayed out into the living room. Back straight. Boobs out. I walked around to the front of the couch with my best come-hither expression on.

Nash was sprawled shirtless on the sofa with the sheet across his lower half. And he was also sound asleep.

I stood for a moment and admired him. His dark hair was like ebony on the yellow of the cushions. He was all lean muscle and perfectly proportioned—not that exaggerated V shape of someone who spent every waking hour doing chest presses at the gym. Slim. Lean. And as my gaze roamed, I realized he was pretty damned perfect. I felt like Goldilocks discovering the perfect man—not too big and not too small, not too hard and not too fluffy. Just right.

Nash made a soft snoring noise then stirred. I smiled, blowing him a kiss. Then I flicked off the light and headed back to my bed.

Soon. We'd just met—well, we'd met before but not more than just seeing each other in passing as each of us did our jobs. We'd been a cross purposes for two years, him there to take a soul while I worked desperately to keep the someone alive. Two years of dancing around each other, trying to figure out what this thing between us was. But tonight was the first night we'd truly had to know each other. There would be plenty of time for sex. There would be our whole lives for sex, however long that was. Tonight? Tonight was for us to settle in together, to feel our way around this new reality, for him to better understand the changes that had happened when he'd sacrificed all he'd ever been to save my sister.

I wanted him, but I wanted this to go at his pace. I didn't want him to ever regret the choice he'd made. And I didn't want to screw this up.

This man...this reaper.... I got the feeling this was forever. I felt at peace with him. I felt like I truly was coming home, warm and safe and protected like I hadn't felt since Grandma had died, and Mom had left. I feared change, but this was a wild crazy change that I knew was going to bring me to a place of joy. This reaper was my future.

And I didn't need a crystal ball or a scrying mirror to know that.

CHAPTER 10

OPHELIA

J had the dream again. This time I awoke to find Nash bent over me, his hands on my shoulders. Without a second thought, I sat up in bed and held him tight. And as the vision receded, I realized that all I had on was a tank top and some underwear, and that I was pressed against Nash's bare chest.

It was a really nice chest. Lean and muscular with just a sprinkling of hair in all the right places. I placed my palm flat over his heart, feeling his pecs jump under my touch. Then, easing back from him, I trailed my fingers down his chest, over taut abs to the waistband of his pants.

And just like that, the nightmare was gone because I was thinking that we needed to go shopping. Nash had only this one outfit, and he'd need more clothes as well as some nice pajama bottoms. I wondered if he was a boxer or a brief guy. I'd ask him, but I could guarantee one hundred percent that his answer would be, "I don't know."

"You had a nightmare?" he asked, wrapping an arm around my waist and scooting me closer.

I shuddered, the images coming back in full color to my

mind. "I've been having this dream lately, but I can't interpret it. Each vision I get another piece of the puzzle, but I worry that by the time I figure it out, it will be too late."

"A prophecy of doom, then?" He leaned forward and nuzzled my neck. Suddenly blood on oleander leaves was the last thing on my mind.

"Yes," I breathed, less because I was answering his question in the affirmative and more because I wanted him to continue trailing little kisses down my neck and across my collarbone like he was doing. "Part of the vision already came true—me on a mountaintop, making a decision where either path led to death."

The kissing stopped. "Last night. Either Sylvie's death or mine. But we weren't on a mountaintop. We were in your eldest sister's house."

"A lot of what happens in a vision is symbolic," I told him. "The hard part is deciding what is symbolic and what is literal. Then interpreting the symbols…. The mountaintop I think meant this was a momentous decision—the choice of Sylvie's physical death or your death as a reaper." I snuggled against his chest. "Did you sleep well?"

"It's the first time I've ever slept. I do feel energized, so I'm guessing I did sleep well." He ran a hand down my back. "After a few hours, I woke and spent the rest of the night reading everything in your house and watching television. Do you know your cable channel has explicit sexual content after midnight? If you have a hot tub and a few willing female friends, I can recreate some of the episodes."

I laughed, lifting my head to look at him. "First, that's pay-per-view, so I hope you didn't run up hundreds of dollars in porn on my cable bill. Secondly, I don't do the group sex thing, and third, I don't have a hot tub."

"I could adapt the episodes to one partner." He leaned

down and kissed my collarbone. "But first I want to hear more about your vision."

I pulled him down onto the bed and snuggled against him, then told him about the vision including the new portion that had appeared in tonight's dream.

"A werewolf?" I felt him chuckle. "And golf balls?"

"The golf balls aren't new. I've got no idea what those are about. The werewolf though…. I recognized her. It was Shelby. She's the first lone wolf in Accident. Cassie put her foot down and insisted that the pack allow her to leave and remain in the town, even though she's now shunned by her pack. She's living under a bridge with Alberta."

"And what does she have to do with blood on oleander leaves, the choice you made last night, this Marcus blaming you for something, a stench on the edge of a forest, and golf balls?"

I shifted around so I was facing him. "Beats me, but as soon as we're done making love, I'm going to get us breakfast and head into town to visit Shelby. Maybe she'll have some idea what the rest of my vision is about."

"After making love?"

There was something really sexy in the deep rumble of his voice. I looked up into his dark eyes. Everything inside me came to life at what I saw there. He might be out of his element, a new mortal, or ex-reaper, or whatever, in this world, but he was learning fast, and the lost confused man of last night had been replaced by one who'd spent hours reading books, perusing soup can labels, and watching a whole lot of porn.

I just hoped it was good porn.

"Too soon? Am I rushing this?" I asked him.

"Well according to the movies I watched, we should be achieving penetrative sexual intercourse less than twenty seconds after meeting for the first time."

"We're way overdue then," I teased. "Seriously though, you've only been an ex-reaper for twelve hours. I'm thinking you might need more than twenty seconds, more than twelve hours."

He smiled. "I've been in love with you since I first saw you two years ago. The last twelve hours has only made those feelings grow stronger. You're strong, caring, compassionate. I've watched you save lives. And last night I saw your love for your family, your comradery with your co-workers. You're an amazing woman, Ophelia Perkins. I want nothing more than to spend whatever this new life is with you, but if you don't feel the same, I understand."

Did I? Feel the same, that is? It's true that I didn't know him well. But I'd certainly gone to bed with men I'd barely known based on sexual attraction alone, and what I felt for Nash was more than just sexual attraction. He'd delayed reaping souls for me. He'd given up everything he was, resurrected my sister, for *me*. In the last twelve hours I'd seen him to be kind, funny, and amazingly resilient. From reaper, to maybe-mortal, he'd accepted this new life of his with remarkable composure.

And the warmth of him here against me was making me really want to move things in a very physical direction.

"Before you answer, I have to confess something," Nash said.

Crap. I held my breath, worried that this was going to be a deal breaker.

"How attached were you to that oleander plant in the kitchen?" His brows knitted with worry as he watched for my reaction.

"You reaped the oleander? I just got that thing two days ago. There's no way I'd managed to almost-kill it in that time. No, this is all on you, buddy. You're a plant murderer. Just admit to it."

His lips twitched. "I swear it was dying. Someone's feline had been peeing into the soil. I'm surprised you didn't smell it."

I stared at him in surprise, then started to laugh. "Marcus. He's a panther shifter. He gave me the plant because he hates them and his intern is turning his office into a jungle. Oh my God, he was peeing in the oleander! Sylvie would have a field day with this passive aggressive shit. I can't believe it!"

"So you're not mad?"

"That you put the oleander out of its misery? No. Although I do think we'll need to take this strange proclivity of yours into consideration when doing job searches. No landscaping jobs. No farming. Produce sales might even be out of the question."

We cuddled tight, laughing and joking about all the careers he should and shouldn't consider. Then we lay together in companionable silence, his hand roaming over my back making my mind think of other things besides resumes and job applications.

He kissed the side of my head. "Sleep. I'll stay here and hold you. I'll keep the nightmares away."

"You can do that?" I looked up at him.

"Heck if I know." He smiled, his hand tracing little circles on my lower back. "I'll do my best."

"What if I don't want to sleep?" I pressed myself against him. "I want you, Nash. I like you here in my house. I like you here in my bed. And I want you."

"Are you sure? Should I pretend to be delivering pizza, or servicing your dishwasher? Should we wait for you to get a hot tub and convince three friends to join you in a hedonistic night of pleasure?"

I snorted. "That's Sylvie, not me. Actually I'm not sure Sylvie's into the three friends thing, although she'd enthusiastically support that option for other people. I just need you.

I need you right here, right now. And maybe a few times more if we're up to it."

His breath caught. "I'm fairly certain I'd be up to it."

My hand traced the warm skin on his ribs, tickling down his side to grip his waistband with a firm tug. "Then let's make love and eat breakfast. In that order."

"Yes, ma'am." He kissed me, scooting my tank top up as I unbuttoned his pants.

We explored each other's bodies, slowly and with great attention. I'd never been with someone so attentive to my needs, so focused on *me*. We stroked, kissed, and tasted. We giggled at missteps, then adjusted and got back on track. And when we got serious and I felt that first orgasm shiver through me, I knew this was the man I wanted in my life forever.

It all felt so right with him, so perfect. Who would have thought that me of all witches would find what might be a forever love in death?

It was like fate. It was like…magic.

* * *

IT WAS close to dinner time before I showered, left Nash to watch television, and headed into town. The drive seemed shorter than usual, and I was well aware that I was smiling the whole way. It wasn't just the sex—which was awesome, by the way—it was everything about Nash. He was sweet and funny, and we'd spent the day eating, watching movies, and going over career options for him as I pulled my laptop out and tried to put together a resume. Not much got done in the way of job searches though, since we were continuously finding ourselves in the bed, or on the couch, or rolling across the floor doing it like rabbits. I'll admit it was the best day ever, and it had been hard to pull myself away, but after seeing Shelby in my dream, I knew I had to come see her.

Nash would be there when I got home. The thought sent happy bubbles of excitement through me.

Parking just off the road, I walked down the embankment to the house the werewolf shared with Alberta, then I knocked on the thick oak door and waited. It only took a few seconds before the door swung open and I found myself face-to-face with Shelby. The werewolf looked…different. Females who were part of the pack were under a whole lot of restrictions as to who they could sleep with, procreate with, and even to some extent their ability to come and go from the compound. The alpha could deny anyone permission to leave the pack territory, but that sort of restriction tended to be placed more on females than males, no doubt to keep them from "accidently" having carnal relations with non-werewolves. Males were allowed to screw any consenting being they chose. Females? No so much.

It sounded strict, and it was, but there were plenty of female werewolves who came and went in the town proper, although they tended to hang with groups of their own kind. Female werewolves weren't meek and placid. They were just as bad-ass as the males and were just as rowdy and short of temper. But when there was a difference of opinion, female werewolves tended to support the males and especially their alpha, knowing that those privileges and freedoms they enjoyed could be yanked away without warning.

It was a culture Cassie was working hard to change. And Shelby had been ground zero for that effort. The werewolf had fallen in love with a troll—a female troll—and gotten caught, warned, and told what the punishment would be if she continued to see her lover, Alberta. The two had gone into stealth mode, but when Clinton had seen them together one night, they'd needed to make a snap decision.

Shelby would have lost her life if it had been up to Dallas, but Cassie had stepped in and the town of Accident now had their first lone wolf. She was shunned by every other werewolf, refused access to the compound, and completely cut off from her family and former pack mates. It was agonizing for her, and I knew she was struggling with the aftermath of that whole thing.

There were some problems I wasn't sure even love could solve, but in my heart, I rooted for Alberta and Shelby to make it. And it *was* a bit easier now that there was one more lone wolf in town—Stanley. He'd been trapped between the two warring alphas and had put his neck on the line to help Bronwyn. Cassie had granted him sanctuary and told both Dallas and Clinton that if anyone so much as growled at the werewolf, she'd set their hide on fire.

Or singe their beards off their faces.

Werewolf politics aside, Shelby looked different. Gone was her typical worn, boot-cut jeans and tank top. Gone was the long, bushy hair. Gone was the faint fuzz of a beard that some of the female werewolves worked diligently to shave while others embraced. Instead, Shelby had on a pale pink skater-skirt that came to mid-thigh paired with a floral-print blouse. Her hair was close cropped into a cap of dark lamb's wool that given werewolf genetics, I knew she had to trim daily. And her face was either freshly shaved, or she'd been using one of the hair-removal products I'd seen advertised on late-night infomercials.

She had on makeup. And that was a shocker because I could count on one hand the number of female werewolves who wore makeup.

"Ophelia." Shelby smiled nervously. Everyone in town tended to be nervous around me, mostly because I was an oracle, but I got the feeling the werewolf had a more personal reason to be stressed about my visit.

"Can I come in?" I asked.

She hesitated then stood aside and opened the door wider. "Alberta's not here right now."

"That's okay. It's you I need to see."

Shelby flinched at that, then fluttered her hands toward the couch. "Sit. Sit. I'll get you a cup of tea. It's herbal—ginger peach. Is that okay?"

"It sounds lovely." I sat and watched her pull two mugs from the cupboard and turn on the kettle. Alberta's place was a cozy timber frame and wattle dwelling under the bridge. The ceilings were low, and there didn't appear to be more than one window in the entire tiny house, but it was neat and clean with bright colors and all sorts of knickknacks on the shelf-lined walls. The house was one room with a kitchenette in one corner and a bed in the back. A little table separated my sofa spot from the two-burner stove and diminutive fridge. Trolls weren't small people by any means, but they liked living in small places. Alberta had once told me it made her feel warm and safe and loved to have four walls close around her and all her possessions within reach.

Watching Shelby fiddle with the tea, I wondered how a werewolf was coping with what to her must feel claustrophobic. I hoped she was shifting and running through the woods on a nightly basis; otherwise, I worried the closeness of the house might affect her mental health.

"Here." Shelby handed me a mug of tea. "Oh! Do you take sugar?"

"No, this is fine." I sipped the tea. "It's lovely." It was. The sweetness of peach and the bite of ginger made for a wonderful combination.

Shelby sat across from me on one of the chairs at the table and stared down at her mug. "Just tell me why you're here. Is Alberta going to cheat on me? Leave me? Kick me out? Is Dallas going to kill me? Am I going to die?"

Oh, the life of an oracle, so welcome everywhere I went.

"Not that I'm aware of," I told her. "I had a vision of a trail of blood that led to your door."

The werewolf paled. "I swear I haven't hurt anyone. Not since the incident with Clinton. I know the rules of this town, and I follow them. I'm not about to get kicked out of the one place that stands between my death at the hands of the pack or living as a human in the outside world, unable to let my wolf run free."

"I didn't get the impression you'd harmed anyone, Shelby," I told her. "There was blood on oleander leaves, something dead at the edge of a woods, and a moonrise on a mountaintop, and...golf balls for some weird reason. In the latest vision, there was a trail of blood leading to your door. It felt like there was someone injured who was coming to you for help."

Shelby picked up her mug and sipped her tea. As she sat the mug back on the table, I saw her hands tremble. "No injured person has come to me for help."

There was truth in her statement, but I could tell she was hiding something from me. And I could tell there was someone she was protecting.

"You know my role in this town, right?" I waited for her nod. "I'm a Perkins. A witch. An oracle. I was born with the sacred duty to serve the residents of this town, to protect them, to keep them safe from whatever may harm them— either from the outside world or within our town wards. I'm afraid, Shelby. I'm afraid that someone is going to die. And I need to do everything I can to prevent that. Help me. Don't let someone's death be my fault. Don't let me fail."

Her hands shook so hard on the mug that the tea slopped over the edge and onto the table. "I can't. I've given my word. It's not my secret to share. I've given my word and I can't tell you."

"Is it Alberta?" I asked. "Is she in trouble? Because I can help. *We* can help."

"No. I can't tell you, Ophelia. I really can't."

It had to be a werewolf. If it wasn't Alberta, then I couldn't imagine anyone else who would be coming to Shelby's door needing her assistance. I closed my eyes, feeling my way through the vision once more. Fear. Fear and desperation. And Shelby represented a safe spot, a home base where whoever this was might find an escape from what was bearing down on him or her.

"Ask them if you have permission to tell me," I pleaded. "I want to help. I *need* to help. I feel as if this person is afraid and doesn't know where to turn to or who to trust, but please let them know that they can trust me. I'll help them."

"And if you can't?" Shelby asked.

I thought of Nash, of my dead plants. I didn't know how far his powers now extended or if he had anything but the most minor of abilities, but perhaps we could bluff.

If a lifetime of being an oracle had taught me anything, it was that people feared death above most anything. And who else could represent that fear better and drive it home than a reaper?

"I promise you I can help, Shelby. I promise."

She stared at me a moment. "I'll...I'll talk to this person and let you know. That's the best I can do, Ophelia."

I drank down the rest of my tea, knowing that would have to be good enough.

CHAPTER 11

OPHELIA

"So...what do you think?"

Nash looked down at the two plates. "Sausage gravy. The chipped beef is good, but I like the sausage gravy better."

I'd brought home pizza last night after meeting with Shelby and we'd had an amazing evening together, but I felt like it was time to get out and expose Nash to more than the limited culinary opportunities in my half-empty fridge. Plus, we needed to check out a few job openings we'd printed out from online ads. As much as I loved cuddling up with the reaper on the couch, holed up in our home, and having sex multiple times a day, I knew we'd need more. *He'd* need more. I went back to work Thursday and would pretty much be at the firehouse for four days straight. Nash needed a purpose. He needed friends. He needed to learn how to drive. And he needed a job.

"I'm more of a chipped beef fan, but you do you." I scooted another plate over to him. "Grits. Love them? Hate them? Thinking you might be able to use them to spackle your drywall in a pinch?"

Nash dropped a pat of butter into the grits and stirred it in with a spoon. "This tastes different than the oatmeal, right?"

He hadn't liked the oatmeal at all, which kind of sucked since it was my go-to breakfast. Although the reaper had learned a lot of basic food prep in the last twenty-four hours. I had no doubt he'd be whipping up omelets and baking biscuits in no time, especially if he got the kitchen assistant job here at the Stagecoach Diner.

"Not a fan." He pushed the grits away and took a quick sip of coffee.

"Heathen." I smiled at him. "Next you'll be telling me you don't like bacon."

"I absolutely *do* like bacon." He reached across the table and took my hand.

I entwined my fingers with his, turning as I heard the chime on the diner's door. Shelby stood in the doorway, her nose twitching as she looked around. Her gaze settled on me and she took a few steps forward, halting abruptly as her attention shifted to Nash.

Her nostrils flared. With a clenched jaw, she kept moving toward our table as if she was having to force her legs to move against their will.

"Sit," I told her, indicating a chair. "He's with me. It's okay."

I wasn't sure what her issue was with Nash. Shelby had always been a bit of a badass as far as werewolves go, but she'd become a whole lot more cautious and wary since becoming a lone wolf. I'm sure it was difficult for someone who was used to having an entire pack at their back to suddenly find themselves on their own and an anathema to their former pack mates.

"What *is* he?" she whispered.

Ah. In a town full of supernatural creatures, Nash must

have been nothing she'd ever smelled before. It was all about the nose with shifters.

"He's…" I paused and looked at Nash, not sure what I should call him. "He's a reaper."

Shelby's eyes widened. "Who's he here for?"

"Me," I joked. "Haven't you ever met a reaper before? With the rate you werewolves kill each other, I would think they'd be a common sight up at the pack compound."

"They're not like this." She motioned toward Nash. "I guess they're incorporeal? We don't sense them. We don't smell them. I didn't even know there really *were* reapers."

"There's no need for us ever to be in physical form," Nash told her. "Or for anyone beyond the person who is dying to be aware of our presence."

"So why are you like this now?" She wrinkled her nose. "You smell kind of like the demons, except more…cold. Kind of like…death."

"He smells like dead things?" I was fascinated by this whole topic of how Nash smelled. To me…well, to me, he smelled damned fine. Warm. Like sunshine on pine needles and hay fields. I remembered how his skin had felt cool when he'd first appeared in Cassie's kitchen, but it wasn't like that now.

"No. Dead things smell wonderful. I mean, not dead werewolves. That's an unnerving kind of smell. Dead prey is one of the best smells there is, but he smells like death. Like cold fire."

I had no idea what cold fire smelled like. I assumed there were all sorts of nuances to aromas that were absolutely beyond my ability to comprehend but were commonplace to shifters like Shelby.

"You said he's here for you?" Shelby shot Nash an uneasy glance. "Not for someone else. There's no one else going to die here, right?"

"Everyone dies eventually," Nash told her. "So yes, everyone here is going to die."

There was a reason reapers were often given the title "grim." As much fun as Nash generally was, any conversation with him that skirted on death was totally a buzzkill. It was "we're all going to die" and "everyone dies" and "eventually you'll be dead." I'd made the decision sometime yesterday that we needed to avoid these topics with Nash, otherwise he would never have friends *or* get a job.

"Yeah, but no one's going to die but Ophelia. Right?"

I scowled, a little miffed that Shelby wasn't the slightest bit alarmed that a reaper might possibly be here for me. Nice to know the werewolf didn't really care whether I died or not. Mortality aside, she was clearly here to see me about something, and she *was* concerned that Nash might be reaping a soul beyond my own. Hers perhaps? Or someone else's?

Someone who would bleed on the oleander leaves?

"He's here for me," I reassured her. "As far as we know, he won't be doing any reaping in the near future, but I'm not positive about that. He has killed what seemed to be two perfectly healthy plants in the last twenty-four hours. Plus, there are other reapers who might show up any time and do their thing."

She dragged her gaze back over my way. "I need to talk to you. Can I…can I speak with you in private?"

I pushed the plate of bacon and eggs to Nash. "Here. Eat up. And when the waitress comes back, ask her to put in an order for the French toast with the cornflakes on it. You've got to try them."

Nash dug in. I got up and followed Shelby outside. And through the parking lot. And down a hill through a small copse of trees to a concrete embankment. For a human, this amount of cloak and dagger would have been excessive, but half the town residents had the sort of hearing that would pick up a whisper at fifty yards, so the distance made sense. It also told me that whatever Shelby was about to confide in me about was something really important. I got the impression it was life-or-death important.

"I got a visit from Tink a couple of weeks ago," she told me.

I waited, and when it became clear she wasn't going to continue, I lifted my hands. "Tink, as in short for Tinkerbell? Is that a new pixie in town or something?"

Shelby rolled her eyes. "No, it's not short for anything. Her name's Tink. She's a werewolf."

I caught my breath. Shelby was a lone wolf. Any members of the pack were forbidden from any contact with her. The only werewolf who would acknowledge her presence was Stanley, because he too was a lone wolf and exiled from the pack.

"I'm assuming Tink is a sister? A cousin?" I imagined it would be hard on family members to be forbidden to talk to each other. Werewolves were a close-knit bunch, and family was very important to them.

"No, she's Ruby's daughter." Shelby hesitated, then must have realized that I didn't know Ruby, either. "She's been mating age for a while now, but she's stayed single. Playing the field, you know. Dallas doesn't push anyone to mate young. He's got his faults, but this ain't one of them. Old Dog Butch used to insist on a mating within the first four heats."

I wasn't sure I wanted to know any of this. "You're talking about Tink, right? Not Ruby?"

"Ruby's mated to Len. They've been together sixty some years. Tink's unmated. And like I said, Dallas don't push us. That's why I was single at my age. If Old Dog Butch would have won the challenge, I'd have been mated with half a dozen pups by now."

I understood, but just because Dallas Dickskin had one redeeming feature, it didn't negate all the asshole things he'd done in his lifetime.

"So, what's up with Tink? She doesn't want to abide by Dallas' mandate to shun you?"

I assumed so, or she wouldn't have come to visit Shelby. I wondered if they'd been close before Shelby left the pack. And I wasn't sure how her being unmated played into this.

Suddenly I was imagining all sorts of scenarios where Alberta and Shelby were in some sort of polyandry relationship and Tink was joining them. It wasn't unheard of here in Accident. Some of our residents embraced what humans would have considered to be unconventional romantic situations. Although, how would Alberta's tiny house hold the three of them? Plus, I'd always got the impression that Alberta was a one-person sort of troll.

"Tink's got a suitor, and Ruby is pushing her to accept, and she doesn't feel like she has any other options," Shelby said. "She knows Cassie will protect her if she leaves the pack and becomes a lone wolf, but she's not sure if she wants to do that, so she came to see me."

"Wait. Dallas doesn't force wolves to mate by a certain age, but he'd let someone force their daughter to mate? Arranged marriages are okay?"

Shelby twisted her hands together. "It's complicated. Our culture says mates are fated, and that the wolf side of us knows who he—or she—is supposed to spend their life with. But in reality, it's different. Males screw around. There's the occasional divorce, although it's very difficult to get that approved, and there's a social stigma against it. Widows and widowers often find a second 'fated mate.' Or a third. Or a fourth if they're very long-lived."

"But arranged marriages? Arranged matings?" I pressed.

"There's a lot of pressure when your parents feel the

mating is advantageous to the family," Shelby explained. "Most of us give in rather than have to live with a family that holds a grudge because we didn't mate with who they wanted. Family is important. It's as important as pack. No one wants to disappoint their parents or the head of their family."

I'll admit my blood was starting to boil at the thought that some werewolf was pressuring her daughter into mating against her wishes. "You did tell her she was welcome to live in Accident as a lone wolf, didn't you?"

Shelby nodded. "But I couldn't sugar coat it. Living away from the pack, not having anyone you grew up with, your friends or family, even acknowledge your existence any longer…. It's hard, Ophelia. I love Alberta, and it's still hard. There's not a day that goes by where I don't wish I couldn't have been given another option, where there would have been the possibility for me to have a troll for my mate and still be a welcome member of my pack."

"What did Tink say?" I asked. "Is she going to leave or stay?"

"She said she'd think about it. I don't know who this suitor is but given the choice of humiliating her family and living her life in exile, Tink might decide to accept the mate. I got love here in town. I got my mate. But if Tink becomes a lone wolf, she'll possibly be giving up having a mate at all or having pups. Her only choice if she wants to mate to a werewolf and have pups in exile is Stanley. And no offense to Stanley, but I doubt he's Tink's type."

I briefly wondered what Tink's type was.

"Could she possibly appeal to Clinton's faction and live there?" I asked. "That way she'd still be part of a pack, and she'd have some options to mate with a werewolf if she decided she wanted to do that."

"That's not easy to do. Werewolves just can't jump back

and forth between packs. Once the division was made, changing packs isn't a simple thing. Plus, she'd be unable to see friends or family ever again. And if there's war, which it looks like that might happen, there's a good chance Clinton's pack will be killed. She wouldn't be spared."

This was all so complicated, but ultimately it needed to be Tink's decision. Cassie was working on changing things in the werewolf packs, but changing laws was far easier than changing centuries of culture. Hopefully one day there would be several pack options for werewolves and a simple process to change packs without fear of being cut off from friends and family. Hopefully one day there would be a thriving group of lone wolves who could come together for hunts or companionship and not suffer the stigma of exile or the feelings of alienation. One day.

But until then, Tink would need to make a choice. All we witches could do was support her if she chose to go against pack culture.

"She was supposed to come visit me last night," Shelby said. "I didn't say anything when you came, because it wasn't my secret and I wanted to keep her trust and her confidence. But she didn't show, and I haven't heard anything from her in the past two days and I'm worried. Maybe she decided to accept the wolf Ruby wants her to mate with and felt it better to not risk seeing me again. That's okay. If that's what happened, then I understand. But I'm worried. I just want to make sure she's okay, and not hurt or locked up somewhere or being forced into something."

"And you obviously can't go up to the compound and check on her."

Shelby shook her head. "I can't even ask about her because none of the werewolves will talk to me. It's not like they're going to talk to an outsider, either—well, an outsider besides a witch. They've got to talk to a Perkins. They've got to answer to you and your sisters."

Now this was all making sense.

She twisted her hands together. "Dallas threatened to put me to death or lock me in the compound and mate me off to whoever he chose because I was fooling around with a troll, but I don't think he'd force Tink to mate against her wishes. It's Ruby I'm worried about."

"So, you want me to go talk to Ruby and ask for Tink? Make sure she's okay and that whatever is happening is her choice?" I asked.

"No, I want you to talk to Dallas. Nobody mates without his approval. He has to do the ceremony. It's binding. It's pack law. It's a union in front of the entire pack. He'd know. And he'd have the power to make Ruby bring Tink to you so she can tell you it's her choice."

"If she's being pressured, then she'll just lie," I reminded the werewolf.

"But you're a witch. You can tell if she's lying, right? You've got spells and wands for that sort of thing, right?"

I didn't have spells and wands for that. Cassie would. Bronwyn might. Not me, though. "Shelby, I'm thinking this might be something Cassie should do rather than me."

"No! I know Cassie is the head witch, but she and Dallas are like two alphas fighting during the full moon. He's not going to be willing to do anything she asks right now, and she'd be liable to get mad and set him on fire or something. Then things will be even worse for Tink. Dallas will know she was talking to me against his mandate. And he'd probably be more liable to mate her off out of spite."

"So what excuse am I to give Dallas for asking about Tink? How do I explain that I know about this proposed mating?"

Shelby shrugged. "You're an oracle. Tell him you divined

it and you're concerned. Tell him you didn't want to go to Cassie, that this might be nothing and you don't want any more bad blood between the witches and the pack. Smooth it over like you always do. Just make sure Tink's okay and doing what she wants."

I sighed, knowing there was no way I could get out of this. "Okay. I'll do it."

"Today?" Shelby pleaded. "I don't know how fast Ruby might push this mating, and once it's done, it's done. Tink's not the sort of wolf to go back on a blood vow. Once the ceremony is done, it'll be too late to stop it."

Shelby's words made me think of something I hadn't considered. "So, what do I do if this Ruby is forcing Tink to mate and she slips me the secret sign or something that she wants out? I can't exactly grab her and take off. What do you expect me to do if she's unwilling and being forced?"

"Tell Dallas he needs to intervene."

"And if Dallas tells me to go get bent?"

Shelby lifted her chin. "Then you go get your sister and have her haul up the mountain with her demon and force them to let Tink go."

Hopefully I wouldn't get killed before I could do that. Maybe it was *my* blood on the oleander that I was seeing in my visions. "Okay. I'll do it."

I didn't think this had anything to do with my disturbing visions, but I couldn't refuse to help Shelby. And I couldn't refuse to help a young werewolf who might be locked away in some cell, beaten or starved until she agreed to mate with whoever her mother wanted.

I headed back inside to see that Nash had not only polished off the eggs and bacon but had already started in on the French toast. We were going to probably have to have a serious talk about portion control sometime. And sharing.

"Hey. Save some of that for me," I teased as I sat and

grabbed a fork. The diner dipped their bread in a milk and egg mixture, then coated it in cornflakes before frying it in butter. The result was something so good it was almost a crime to put syrup on it.

Almost.

"Is there a problem with the werewolf?" Nash asked, spearing another piece of buttery goodness.

I glanced around the diner, realizing that I'd need to be circumspect. None of the patrons were werewolves at the moment, but there were three banshees over in the corner and they were incredible gossips with darned good hearing.

"She just wanted a weather divination for Alberta's tomato seedlings. Common practice is to put them in the ground the weekend of Mother's Day, but we've had some late frost in the past few years. No one wants to lose their seedlings to a cold snap."

Nash shot me an odd look. "It's June. She's getting a weather divination for next year?"

"Yes." The tomato thing was a total lie, but in all honesty, I probably *should* do a weather divination. No doubt people would be asking me for it soon anyway. It might be June, but people liked to plan, and everyone always wanted to know how much snow to expect this winter and when to put their bulbs in the ground. I liked to do a big Farmer's Almanac kind of thing once a year. Might as well get started on that in the next few weeks.

I fiddled with my coffee cup. "Something came up, and I've got a quick errand I need to run. I know you were going to apply for a few more jobs, but maybe we can do that later?"

Nash gave me a long, searching look. "I take it I'm not going with you on the errand?"

I was torn. I liked having Nash around. Something in me felt warm and settled when he was nearby. And reaper or not, having backup at the werewolf compound wouldn't be a bad thing. But it was important for this visit to appear casual and routine, and Shelby's reaction to Nash gave me pause. Dallas most definitely did not like Lucien or Hadur. I got the feeling showing up at his door with Nash would set his hackles up just as much as if I'd arrived with a demon in tow. It was kind of like visiting with half a dozen loaded guns strapped to my sides. Not a good way to start off what I hoped would be a friendly, non-confrontational conversation.

Besides, what was the risk? I might be an oracle and lacking in both offensive and defensive spells, but I was still a Perkins and that commanded respect. It would be a quick visit. Meet with Dallas. Confirm that Tink was not being chained in a dungeon somewhere and that her wishes were being respected. Leave.

Easy peasy.

"Do you mind?" I asked Nash. "It's kind of an oracle witch thing. I shouldn't be too long. I'll be back sometime in the afternoon."

"Should I wait at your house?" He stabbed a few more pieces of French toast and I realized if I didn't get my fork in there, there soon wouldn't be any left.

"Yes...no, wait." Drat. If I drove Nash back to my house in the complete opposite direction of the mountain the were-wolves called home, it would waste hours of my time. And a lot of gas. "How about you stay in town? Shopping? I can give you some money and you can explore. And you can go ahead and apply for those other jobs now that you know how to fill out the applications."

He nodded, scooping the last piece of French toast up on his fork. "Sure. I might go over to the fire department to visit with your co-workers afterward and wait there for when you get back. They were nice."

I smiled, thrilled that Nash and my co-workers had gotten along so well.

A reaper among rescue workers. It was an odd image, but Nash really did need to have friends in town. Maybe he'd enjoy training to become an EMT. Or open a bakery. Or grow the most amazing tomato garden ever.

I thought about my dead plants and realized we should probably nix that option. At least with the kitchen assistant job at the diner or the other openings we'd circled, he wouldn't have to worry about accidently reaping something or someone.

"Here." Nash held his fork out with the last bit of French toast on it. "You have the last piece."

I leaned forward and let him feed it to me, enjoying the sweetness of syrup, the crunch of cornflakes, the eggy flavor of the bread. My eyes met his and he smiled.

His expression was warm, kind, and there was such affection in his eyes that my heart lurched.

CHAPTER 12

OPHELIA

I pulled up to the compound and parked. A few werewolves were milling about outside the main house. I knew my presence wasn't a surprise. With Clinton vying for control of the pack, Dallas probably had sentries posted all over his side of the mountain. These werewolves hanging out right now were curious onlookers because I would hardly be viewed as a threat.

Either way, I nodded as I passed them, recognizing a few. I'd grown up in Accident and knew just about every one of the residents, but there were always a few here and there that lived more of a hermit life, or ones that I didn't run across on a regular basis. I'd say I knew about eighty percent of Accident's residents.

I only knew about twenty percent of the werewolf residents inside our wards. It was a bit embarrassing to admit that, but they were a secretive bunch and quite a few of them never ventured off the mountain, let alone came into town. In school, I'd only had one or two werewolf classmates. Most of them were educated in schools within the pack compound. The only ones attending the public schools of

Accident were children of the most accepting of werewolf parents. Pack. Family. Territory. Those were the priorities, and outsiders weren't to be trusted much more than those humans living beyond the wards.

I agreed with Cassie that this had to stop. It was a travesty that none of our witch ancestors had either the power or the inclination to bring the werewolves into the fold. Other shifters kept their culture and traditions but were active members of our community. There was no reason the werewolves could do the same.

I knocked on the front door and waited, knowing that the delay in answering was a power play. I was two seconds from pulling out my nail file and doing an impromptu manicure when the door swung open and I found myself face-to-face with a female werewolf.

Parlay. I knew her. She'd actually been one of the werewolves who'd attended school down in the town, and she was a few years older than me. Bronwyn was probably in her class. She looked exactly the same as she had in high school, but then again, werewolves were a long-lived group and tended to age exceptionally well. Her dark hair was shoulder length—shorter than most of the other wolves and probably requiring weekly trims—and she didn't have the facial hair that both genders of werewolves tended to sport. Males had all sorts of varieties of beards depending on their notions of style, but they were rarely clean shaven. Females had softer, peach-fuzzy facial hair that could be thick along the jawline or a faint shadow on their lower face. Young female werewolves tended to shave their faces, although not their body hair. I think the face-shaving was more from having to blend in with humans than as a way to keep from appearing unfeminine to non-werewolves. Older females—those who were long mated and had several pups—embraced their furry faces with an enthusiastic defiance that I admired. I had no problems with anyone's grooming choices, but I hated to think a female wolf would feel pressured into shaving to fit in with what they thought the outside world considered feminine and beautiful.

Lots of supernatural races had scales, and leathery hides, and fur. I agreed with all definitions of beauty including a furry female chin.

"Hey, Par," I greeted the werewolf. "Is Dallas in?"

"Ophelia." She stood aside and motioned for me to enter. "I'll let him know you're here. Come into the living room. Can I get you something to drink? Or eat?"

Werewolves weren't rude, but this was far more hospitality than they usually extended to unplanned visitors to the compound.

"I'm good, thanks. How have you been?"

She smiled over her shoulder as she led the way. "Great. I mated two years ago and am expecting a pup this fall."

I offered congratulations, my eyes drifting to her flat stomach. Werewolves. They never showed until the last month.

The living room was full of cushiony leather sofas, the walls lined with deer heads. Parlay turned and lifted her head as she let out a plaintive howl, the sound trailing off on a low note at the end. Then she went over to a cabinet and pulled out a decanter of what looked to be whisky, pouring a splash into two glasses.

"I know you said you didn't want anything, but your visit gives me an excuse to dip into Dallas' good stuff." She handed me a glass. "It's rude to let guests drink alone. Cheers."

"Cheers." Another thing about werewolves—they were perfectly fine drinking during pregnancy. There were plenty of other substances a pregnant or lactating wolf needed to avoid, but alcohol wasn't one of them.

I tossed down the whisky, feeling the warm burn and the peaty aftertaste. Dallas did have some good stuff.

"So, did you guys have a good hunt last moon?" I cradled the glass, figuring I might as well make conversation while I waited for Dallas to make his dramatic appearance.

"I had first blood on a deer, so I'd call it a good hunt."

I toasted her with the glass, even though it was empty. She took that as an invitation to refill both mine and hers. I'd need to be careful. Driving drunk down the steep and narrow roads of Heartbreak mountain wasn't advisable.

"So, who'd you mate with?" I asked, sipping the whisky.

"Beaker." She shot me an impish look over the top of her glass. "Submissive as hell, just like I like 'em. He worships the ground my little paws tread on. It's all 'Yes, Par. Anything you say, Par. Can I please have sex tonight, Par?' That wolf does foreplay like his life depended on it. Which it does."

I hid a smirk, because I could tell she was absolutely besotted with her mate. I was pretty sure the worshiping went both ways, although Parlay would never admit it.

"You got yourself a mate yet, Ophelia?"

There was a note of pity in her voice. I knew lots of the residents of Accident didn't understand why we Perkins witches had remained unattached for so long. Most of us dated, but rarely indulged in an actual relationship. The closest any of us had ever come to that was when Cassie had been in her tumultuous fling with Marcus and that human Adrienne dated that she'd never introduced to anyone. Of course that all changed when Cassie had met Lucien, and Bronwyn had met Hadur.

Hopefully it had changed for me as well.

"I think I might have a mate," I told Parlay. "I'm not positive yet."

"Well, I'm praying for you." The werewolf looked over to

DEBRA DUNBAR

the doorway, then quickly refilled her glass. I realized why a few seconds later when Dallas strode into the room.

The alpha had a presence that, in my opinion, his son Clinton completely lacked. He was tall, powerfully built, with long, silver hair that was pulled back with a leather tie. His reddish-blonde beard was trimmed to about three inches—a departure from the long beard he usually sported. His blue eyes were sharp, and they eyed me from the top of my head to the tip of my toes, then back up again, lingering on my chest.

Dallas Dickskin was a letch. And I was well aware that if I got within a foot of him, he'd probably pinch my ass or grope me. Which is one of the reasons I kept my distance.

"Ophelia." He pronounced my name with a sort of oily drawl. "To what do I owe this pleasure?"

The werewolves might cling to their culture and their own pack law, isolating themselves more than any of the other residents in Accident, but they weren't uneducated. It was never wise to underestimate them or assume that because of their ways, they were ignorant hicks.

"I was hoping you could help alleviate a concern of mine," I said.

I watched him cross to the cabinet and pour himself a whisky, raising the decanter to offer me more. When I declined, he turned to Parlay and frowned.

I'd never seen a werewolf move so fast. With an apologetic glance, she fled the room. Her half-full glass was on the table and she was out the door before I could take a breath.

"I'm always happy to help a Perkins," Dallas told me with a smile that was very close to a leer.

"I'm glad to hear that." I took a sip of my whisky, trying to decide how to best word my inquiry. "For want of a better term, this is a welfare check. I'm here to make sure that a female werewolf named Tink is okay and to speak with her a moment in private."

"When do witches perform welfare checks on were-wolves? We're allowed autonomy, just as the sylphs, and centaurs, and other beings of Accident. Unless you've got a particular reason for wanting to check on one of my pack, then I'm gonna have to refuse your request." The leer was gone from Dallas' face, replaced by an expression that was a mixture of wary and pissed off.

I backpedaled, relying on the only reason I could give for my request. "I had a vision, and I'm concerned for her well-being."

Dallas blanched. And that absolutely revealed how unset-tling my comment was. The alpha had a darned good poker face, and I could probably count on one hand the number of times I'd seen him thrown off his game. This was one.

"Tell me the details of this vision," he demanded.

"Blood on oleander leaves. A full moon on a mountain-top. The odor of a corpse at the edge of the woods. A path of blood to a werewolf's door. And golf balls."

He blinked. "Golf balls?"

"I'm not really sure if the golf balls are part of the divina-tion or not," I confessed.

He shook his head and took another belt of whisky, turning his back on me to refill the glass. "I'm not under-standing how all that relates to you needing to check on Tink."

And *here's* where I lied and hoped the werewolf couldn't tell. "She's at a crossroads. She has a choice to make, and she's upset and feeling pressured. There's fear, and threats, and none of the choices are what she wants."

Dallas snorted and turned back to face me. "That's life. Hell, there's no need to do a welfare check 'cause a were-wolf's struggling to make a decision."

"I feel that the blood in my vision is hers, that the odor of a corpse at the edge of the woods might be her."

He caught his breath, his hand tightening on the glass of whisky. "Her life is in jeopardy?"

It was my turn to blink in surprise. I'd seen Dallas in a lot of situations over the years, and although he cared about the safety and welfare of his pack as a whole, he wasn't all that attached to the individual members. His reaction to the idea that Tink might be hurt or dead—or would soon be hurt or dead—made me suspicious that he knew the female were-wolf *was* in some danger.

"Yes. Her life is in jeopardy. That's my interpretation of the vision."

I might not have much breadth in my witchy abilities. I might not be able to set someone's pants on fire, or enchant a tent stake, or craft a good-luck charm, or create healing potions, or make insects do my bidding or raise the dead, but in some ways my talents garnered more respect than those of my sisters'. Everyone was wary of a witch who could predict the future—especially if they thought my gift might reveal when and how they, or someone else, might die.

Dallas drank down the whisky and set the glass aside. "Tink is fine. I can assure you that she's fine. I'll make sure she's safe and that no harm comes to her. I appreciate you giving me the heads-up on a potential tragedy. My pack is my responsibility, and I'll take special precautions to make sure your prediction doesn't come to pass."

I cut right through that bullshit and came to the point. "I want to see her."

He shook his head. "That's not necessary. Again, I appreciate the warning. I'll take it from here."

I took a step toward Dallas, risking an ass pinch or a grope to bring my point home. "I had a divination. I need to see her and speak with her privately."

"She's not available right now. I'll handle this. You have my word. If you're truly concerned or have any more visions, come back next week and I'll arrange for you to see her then."

This was when I lost my temper. I took another two steps and actually poked Dallas Dickskin, the werewolf alpha, in the chest with my index finger. "What did you all do to her? Lock her in a dungeon until she agreed to mate with who you want? Beat her until she complied? Threaten her? Is that why you won't let me see her? You don't want me to see her bruises or cuts? You don't want her to tell me you're keeping her a captive against her will?"

Dallas snarled and knocked my finger away. "You're crazy. I know you witches have got a problem with how we do things here in the pack, but we're not monsters. Those who violate pack law get locked up and punished, not females who don't want to mate. We don't do that—least not since Old Dog Butch. *I* don't do that."

"Then let me see her," I demanded.

"No." The alpha glared at me.

"Let me see her, or I'll go get Cassie."

From the look in his eyes, I could tell I'd said the wrong thing. Crap, was I the one who was going to end up in a dungeon? He wouldn't dare. Shelby knew I was coming up here and would sound the alarm if I hadn't gotten back to her in twenty-four hours. Cassie would burn them all to ash if they harmed me. Plus, I'd told Nash when we'd left the diner where I was going, and if I didn't come back at this afternoon to pick him up at the firehouse, he'd haul up here and reap every one of these wolves until they let me free.

Or at least reap their non-viable plant life.

It was as if Dallas were thinking the same things, minus Nash killing their begonias, as I was. He let out a breath and looked up to the ceiling, shaking his head.

"I can't let you see Tink," he told me. "She's gone. She ran off last night and hasn't come back yet."

I caught my breath. "The vision...she could be dead. We need to sound the alarm, to scour the mountain. Have you sent out search parties? Sent someone over to see if she defected to Clinton's group? I'll spread the word in Accident and we'll see if anyone in the town has seen her."

Dallas shook his head. "We haven't done anything. Ruby didn't tell me until a few hours ago. She's embarrassed about it. It shames her that this has happened. She's hoping that Tink is just acting out and will be back this afternoon, or maybe by tonight."

"What if she's not?"

"I'll take care of it," he assured me. "We don't want to cause Ruby any undue humiliation. Turning the mountain and the town upside down and sending out alarm will just make things worse. I'll handle it myself."

"I had a vision," I insisted. "A vision with something dead and blood. This is serious, Dallas. It's not just a wolf who got drunk in town and decided to sleep it off in a ditch. She could be in real trouble. She could be dead."

Why was Dallas holding back on this? I could tell he was upset and worried, but for some reason he wanted to keep it all hush-hush.

"I'll take care of it, I swear," he promised me. "Don't disrespect our culture, Ophelia. Ruby is one of ours and I want to spare her any embarrassment. Of course we wouldn't force a law-abiding werewolf to mate against his or her will, but promises are often as binding as the actual mating ceremony. This is a delicate situation. Ruby received an offer from a suitor she felt was perfect for her daughter. She's justified in encouraging the match, and Tink accepted the offer."

"If she accepted willingly, then why did she run off?" I

demanded. "She was pressured into it. She's feeling like she had no choice. That's not a binding promise, Dallas."

The werewolf let out a breath. "It was willing. I promise you that. Very willing. It's just…Tink has always been impulsive and…a whole lot of odd. Her running off like this is an overreaction. She's just got a case of cold paws. This isn't something that rises to the level that the Perkins witches need to be involved with."

His speech made sense, and it was delivered with an incredible honesty that didn't include any ass pinches, or boob grabs, or crotch gropes. I hesitated, thinking of Shelby's worry but weighing that against the fact that this could be a werewolf who'd just decided to take off into the human world for a while.

It might be a temporary case of cold feet, as Dallas had said. Or cold paws.

"Okay," I told the alpha. "Okay, but know that I'm watching, and if she comes to us needing sanctuary or wants to leave the pack, then we're going to support her."

CHAPTER 13

I didn't leave the werewolf compound and go straight to the firehouse and pick up Nash. No, instead I drove the circuitous route around narrow rocky lanes to the back side of the mountain and the tiny bit of territory that Clinton Dickskin had seized from his father. The last mile I was accompanied by three wolves who ran beside my car, signaling my arrival with a series of yips and howls. By the time I pulled into the makeshift metal gates, Clinton was waiting for me.

As much as I agreed with the concept that werewolves should be able to form multiple packs and have their choice of leadership, I really didn't get the appeal of hitching your wagon to Clinton Dickskin. Where Dallas was smooth-talking, strong, and exuded a sort of raw leadership, Clinton came across as a spoiled bully. He spent his free time prowling around the taverns of Accident with a handful of his buddies, drinking booze, playing pool, and getting in fights. The only thing he had going for him in my opinion was that he wasn't a skeevy lecherous pig like his father was.

I noted right away that while Cassie had burned the

werewolf's beard off, he wasn't making serious inroads into growing it back. He should have had at least a few inches of whiskers by now with the way werewolves grew hair. Instead Clinton was sporting a five o'clock shadow.

"Changing the personal appearance up a bit," I commented as I climbed out of the car.

Clinton stepped forward to hold the door for me, which nearly caused me to pass out in shock. Werewolves extended courtesies to their own, but not generally to others. Either Clinton was making efforts to change, or he wanted something from me, and this was an attempt to ingratiate himself.

Or perhaps Cassie's little discussion and beard-burning visit had made him decide he needed to be extra nice to the witches.

"Kinda feels good to be bare-faced." He rubbed a hand over the stubble. "At least it was bare-faced this morning. I might decide all the shaving is more trouble than it's worth."

Huh. A clean-shaven male werewolf. That was an unusual choice. I wondered how much of it really *was* Clinton's decision. Cassie had burned his beard off, but I wouldn't put it past her to have asked Sylvie for a hex to keep Clinton from growing it back. Sylvie tended to stick to the luck side of spells, but I wouldn't fault her for casting a hex like this. The werewolf's scheme last month could have killed Bronwyn.

"It looks nice," I told him. "You should keep it up."

He blushed, which was even more noticeable with the lack of facial hair. It was then I realized Clinton was a good-looking guy. I guess some werewolves looked better with the beards and some better without. Clinton was clearly one of the latter.

"I don't got much in the way of hospitality to offer you." He led the way to a sprawling hacienda-style house that was so new I could practically smell the fresh-cut lumber.

"No worries. I'm actually looking for a female werewolf named Tink and wondering if you'd seen her."

He shot me a puzzled frown, then opened the door and stood aside for me to enter. "She's not one of my pack. If you're looking for Tink, you'd best head up the road to the compound."

I hesitated for a moment, admiring Clinton's décor. The split in the werewolf pack had taken place a few months ago. In that time, they'd managed to build this lodge and a handful of adjoining cabins, put up fencing and gates, built roads, and pee around the perimeter of what they were calling their territory.

Yeah. Pee. Because werewolves were obsessed with urinating around stuff. I was pretty sure the first thing Shelby had done after moving in with Alberta was go pee around the bridge and their home. And I was sure she "refreshed" it all weekly or after a serious rain.

In addition to the necessities, Clinton's pack had also managed to outfit the lodge with a nice selection of curtains, rugs, inexpensive futons, and a papasan that all obviously came from a mish-mash of discount stores but were also obviously chosen with care and an eye to color coordination. Either Clinton had decorating skills that had previously gone unnoticed, or he had a member of his pack who should be on HGTV. The wide open space was a pleasing array of burgundy, navy, and gold southwestern-style prints. I liked it. I liked it a lot.

But I wasn't here to admire the rugs; I was here to find a missing werewolf.

"I was already up at Dallas' place," I told Clinton. "Tink isn't there. She hasn't been there since before last night."

Clinton shrugged. "Could have gone out on a long solo hunt. Or drinking in town. Or maybe she found herself a troll to have sex with."

I refused to respond to that last bit, knowing that Clinton held quite a grudge against Shelby and Alberta. It wasn't just the troll/werewolf relationship that set his hackles up, it was that Shelby had attempted to kill him to keep the relationship a secret.

"Is Tink the type to want to go lone wolf?" I asked instead. "Maybe she decided she wanted to leave the pack, and they're punishing her and pretending that she's just missing overnight?"

Clinton laughed. "There'd have to be something pretty serious for Tink to even think about going it alone. She's very pack-loyal. I can't see her ever being happy on her own or even in a smaller pack like mine. She likes the power of being with a large group. Plus, if they were punishing her and she were in solitary, Dallas would tell you—or tell you it was none of your damned business. He wouldn't give you some story of her being gone. She's probably just hunting."

"I did a divination, and signs point to her being in trouble," I insisted. "Call it a welfare check, but I'm concerned."

Clinton squinted. "What exactly *was* your vision?"

"Blood on leaves. Something dead. Moon on the mountain. Blood in a path to a werewolf's door. Golf balls." I waved away the golf balls at his incredulous look. "I got the impression that Tink was being pressed into a mating she didn't want, that her mother was giving her an ultimatum about accepting this werewolf suitor. In my vision, she was considering becoming a lone wolf to avoid mating with this wolf and her refusal to do so was putting her life in danger."

Clinton slowly shook his head. "Look, Tink's always had delusions of grandeur. She's a strong wolf. Little tiny thing, but dominant as all get out. Human girls dream of marrying princes; well, werewolf girls dream of marrying the pack alpha."

"Little werewolf girls dream of marrying Dallas?" Ugh.

Gross. I mean, the guy was powerful, but he wasn't exactly young and dashing.

"Or me." Clinton gave me a sheepish grin. "It was always assumed I'd eventually win a challenge and take over the pack, although pack alpha isn't necessarily a father-son thing. Dallas beat out Old Dog Butch over six of Butch's sons. I've had plenty of female werewolves indicate that they were interested in being my mate."

"Why didn't you accept one?" It was surprising that Clinton was single at his age. Mating didn't mean sexual fidelity for male werewolves, and it did lend an air of stability for a male wolf to have a mate.

He shrugged. "Not like you'll believe it, but I'm holding out for my fated mate."

I blinked at him, unsure whether he was lying or not.

"I don't want to be in a loveless mating like my father and mother were," he continued. "It was all business for them. Mom didn't care that Dallas slept around. Actually, she preferred it because then he wasn't sniffing her way. There's a reason I was an only pup. They got along okay, but they were happy being pretty much strangers living under the same roof. I don't want that. I want to have a woman by my side that I love. Someone who wants the same things I do. Someone who I can't wait to see every night, who I love waking up next to every morning. I know every female werewolf on the mountain. I've broken bread with them, I've hunted on four legs beside them, hell, I've slept with a good number of them. Not one of them is my fated mate. If it means I stay single my whole life, then I will. I ain't settling for less."

Wow, that speech was just as surprising as Clinton's rather attractive beardless face, and the matching rugs and throw pillows that I was beginning to suspect he had picked out himself.

"But back to Tink…" I sat on the couch, realizing this might be more than a quick visit. "Is there someone she was in love with? Someone she wanted to mate with that her mother or Dallas wouldn't approve of? Maybe her mother put her foot down and told her she needed to accept this other suitor or else?"

Clinton sat across from me on the giant papasan. "I doubt Tink's in love with anyone. If she was, she would have gone off and drug him down the aisle by his beard. And where I can see Ruby getting fed up with it all and insisting she accept a mate of her choice, Tink's not the sort of wolf to bow down to pressure from her mother. Besides, all she'd have to do is go to Dallas and he'd tell Ruby to back off. My father's got his faults, but he don't pressure anyone to mate. I think that's the one thing he learned from being with my mother—an emotionless or one-sided mating is sorta like hell."

"There's no one in the pack she wanted?" I was having trouble jiving Clinton's description of the werewolf with Shelby's tale of a nervous woman thinking exile was preferable to her mother's choice of a mate.

"Me? Dallas?" He laughed. "I didn't really hang around Tink much, even when I was still at the compound, but she was ambitious."

I sat for a moment, trying to sort this all out. There was a suitor Tink didn't want, one that her mother was pushing on her. And if she was considering going lone wolf, that meant Dallas wouldn't support her refusal, even though everyone insisted he was against unwilling matings.

She was gone, her mother worried enough to go to the pack alpha, yet Dallas wasn't sending out the alarm that Tink was missing.

Something tingled through me, a strange and somewhat icky vision.

"What if Dallas is the suitor?" I mused. "What if your father offered for Tink? Her mother would be over the moon for the match. Tink would feel she couldn't say 'no' and insult her own pack alpha. She would have no choice but to accept him or go lone wolf. And if she'd vanished, Dallas would be too humiliated to send out a search party. How embarrassing to be an alpha with a reluctant runaway bride."

Clinton's eyes widened. Then he began to laugh. "*That* would be funny. I can see my father doing it, too. Mating, that is. After my mother died, I'd figured he was thrilled to be single and that he'd stay that way until he died, but with me breaking off into my own pack…"

I knew where Clinton was going with this. Things were simmering just below the surface on Heartbreak Mountain. If the two packs couldn't work things out, and they went to war, Dallas would most likely have to kill his only son. And while pack alpha wasn't an inherited position, there was some expectation that the son of the alpha would eventually take over.

"So, you're thinking your father would want to mate and have a pup to inherit if you end up dead or exiled?" I asked.

Clinton nodded, his mirth evaporating. "Guess that means he isn't thinking we'll be able to work things out peacefully, then. Tink's young, at the age of peak fertility. She's smart and organized. She's strong and dominant. She'd be good at being the alpha's mate. And she's a looker with a hell of a figure. Dad wouldn't shy away from screwing Tink on the regular. He could mate with her, father ten or twelve pups, and still have as many side pieces as he wanted."

I winced, realizing this scenario made the most sense. Would Dallas kill Tink to cover up his embarrassment at being refused? Claim it was a hunting accident? Blame a fictional rival werewolf for being jealous and make some random pack member pay the price?

"Only one problem with that," Clinton commented. "If Dallas offered for Tink, she wouldn't say no. That's every female werewolf's dream, and I know Tink isn't any different. If Dallas came a-calling, she would have hustled his ass down the aisle at lightspeed."

"Unless she'd fallen in love," I mused. "Maybe she used to dream of being the alpha's mate, but someone else caught her eye. And let's face it, her mother isn't going to let her say 'no' to Dallas so she can mate with some other wolf. And I doubt your father would take rejection well."

"No, he wouldn't." Clinton thought for a moment, stroking the stubble where his beard used to be. "I don't think Tink was lifting her tail for anyone, but I've been gone a bit and didn't pay much attention to pack romance while I was there. Could be. Although if it was known she was sweet on someone, Dallas would never have offered for her."

"So maybe it was a fledgling romance and wasn't widely known?" I conjectured. "Or maybe it was with someone outside the pack? One of the other shifter breeds?"

"Or a troll?" Clinton laughed. "I doubt it. If Tink's in love, it's probably with a werewolf. That's just how she rolls."

I stood, then waited for the werewolf to struggle out of the papasan to walk me to the door. "Can you send me a message if you hear anything? I'm really worried about her."

Clinton nodded. "I will, although there's a good chance I won't hear anything. Stanley was my spy with the pack, and now that he's gone lone wolf, I ain't got nobody feeding me information."

I doubted that, but I thanked him anyway. He opened the door for me, walked me to my car, then even had the gallantry to open my car door. Was Clinton Dickskin finally growing up? I hoped this was a sign of things to come for him. I hoped it meant maybe, just maybe, we could have peace on the mountain and more socialization between the werewolves and the other residents of Accident.

Clinton paused before shutting my car door. "So... you think I look better without the beard?" He ran a hand over his bristly cheek. "Really?"

I looked over at the werewolf and felt something stir in my middle, that feeling of butterflies I got when I had a very particular sort of vision. I couldn't quite see who, but I got the feeling that Clinton might just find that fated mate he'd been holding out for.

"Yep. You're looking mighty handsome," I told the were-wolf. "I recommend you keep shaving."

He blushed bright red and looked down for a moment. When he glanced up again, there was a vulnerability in his eyes that I'd never seen before.

"Thanks, Ophelia. Safe travels."

He shut the door and as I pulled out of the compound, I looked back to see him rubbing his chin with a sheepish grin on his face.

CHAPTER 14

NASH

The moment Ophelia drove off in her car, I felt a sense of loss. But even I knew that to hold her too tight would be to kill this fragile growing thing between us. So, I watched until I could see her car no more, then I headed over to the only hotel in town, filled out an application, and asked for Hollister.

The man showed me around, telling me the various housekeeping duties the part-time job entailed, then shook my hand and told me he'd call me. Actually, he'd be calling Ophelia since I didn't have a cell phone yet.

Yesterday had been like heaven—at least what I'd always thought heaven was. Outside of Ophelia's quick trip into town, we'd spent the day in the little paradise of her house, snuggling together, talking, watching movies, eating. Making love. But now the reality of my situation hit me like when I'd turned the wrong knob in the shower and gotten sprayed with ice cold water. I had no phone. I had no clothes beyond what was on my back. I had no money, nowhere to live, nothing to eat beyond what Ophelia generously provided for me. I had no transportation and didn't even know how to drive a car. I was completely dependent on Ophelia and I knew that wasn't good for a relationship.

The waitress at the diner had told me when she'd dropped off the French toast that she was pretty sure I had the assistant cook job. I got the impression this Hollister might also be making me an offer. I had one more place to fill out an application, and if luck went my way, I would hopefully have a job by the end of the week. Ophelia could talk all she wanted about fulfilling careers, but I'd worry about that later and take whatever I was offered—whether it was cleaning bathrooms and changing sheets, frying eggs and slicing potatoes, or whatever this other job might entail. I didn't have the luxury of waiting to figure out my dream career. That could come after I'd made enough money so Ophelia wasn't having to pay for everything.

Leaving the hotel, I explored the town. There were clothing shops with outfits to cover all sorts of bodies with any number of appendages. With the money Ophelia had given me, I bought a few shirts and pants, then continued on down Main Street, checking out art galleries, furniture stores, a pharmacy, and a florist.

Besides the basil and oleander plant, I'd reaped two boxwoods, a sugar maple sapling, and an entire row of peony bushes since yesterday. I might be as Ophelia liked to call a "retired reaper," but clearly, I still had my abilities at least when it came to plant life. That realization had definitely played into what job opportunities I could pursue. Landscaping jobs were completely out, as was anything involving horticulture.

I forced myself to keep away from the florist, even thought I could tell that some of his asparagus ferns were not long for this world, and kept walking to the edge of the town. Next to a coffee shop that tantalized me with its aroma was a jewelry shop.

Mirabelle Jewelry. I looked at the list Ophelia and I had made together to confirm this was the place, then went on in.

Inside, a fairy examined a tray of earrings, her iridescent wings vibrating behind her as she sorted the sparkling gems. Her skin was a luminous gray, her pink lips parting to show a row of sharp teeth as she smiled at me.

"A reaper." Her voice rang like windchimes. "What does an agent of death want with baubles from the earth?"

"I'm actually here about the job you posted," I told her.

Her eyes widened, her mouth dropping open. "Job?"

I pulled out the piece of paper. "Sales clerk?"

She stared at me for a moment. "Do you know anything about fine jewelry?"

I looked down at the trays in their glass cases, chains and rings of metal with sparkling gems. "Is it something I can learn?"

She pulled something from the case and held it up. "What's this?"

"A ring?" Was this a trick question?

"The stone. What's the stone?"

I peered closer. It was colorless but cut in angles that reflected the light and made it appear to sparkle. "Glass?"

She sighed and put the ring back. "Perhaps you should stick to being a reaper."

I opened my mouth to tell her I'd been fired, then remembered that I needed to word it differently. "I'm on a bit of a sabbatical and am looking for part time or full time work."

She wrinkled her tiny button nose. "Reapers take sabbaticals? And they don't give you all some sort of stipend for when you're on leave?"

"No. It's okay if I'm not qualified for this position," I assured her. "I'm confident that either the job at the diner or the one cleaning bathrooms and changing sheets at the hotel will come through."

"There's got to be a better option for you." She tapped a long silver nail on her lower lip. "You should talk to Sheriff Oakes. I'll bet he'd be thrilled to have a reaper as a deputy or maybe you could be a bailiff at the courthouse. Nobody would mess with you. They'd all run when they saw you coming. And if they didn't behave, them *bam*. Dead. It's a job that would take advantage of your natural talents."

It was an excellent idea. I took out the piece of paper and made a quick note. "Ophelia and I didn't see any job openings online in law enforcement but that's an excellent suggestion. Right now, I'll take whatever I'm offered, but perhaps I can look into this as a long-term option."

"Ophelia?" She motioned for me to lean over the glass case. As I did, she reached out and ran her silver nails down my cheek, her light blue eyes staring into mine. "You are Ophelia's."

"Yes. I'm Ophelia's." I didn't hesitate at all because it was absolutely true.

"Pity." She smiled. "I have no wish to anger one of the Perkins witches by inviting you back to my house later. But perhaps this is an opportunity. Let me show you some rings."

"I don't have any money, and I have no need for adornment," I told her.

The stones and metals *were* aesthetically pleasing, and from hours watching late-night informercials, I knew there were humans in particular who valued these things and were motivated to quickly purchase them before time ran out and the low-low introductory price had ended. Humans and dragons. And goblins. And gnomes. And trolls. Okay, all beings, mortal and immortal, liked sparkly shiny things, it seemed.

"Not for you, reaper." She pulled out a tray and sat in front of me. "Maybe soon you will have money because I believe that in the near future you will want to purchase something like this beautiful diamond solitaire."

"I'd rather purchase a cell phone and maybe a few packets of underwear," I told her.

She let out a huff, then waved the ring in front of my face. "This is better than cell phones and underwear. It's for you to give to your loved one, as a pledge of fidelity and partnership for all eternity."

"Why do I need a ring for that?" This was all so confusing —more confusing than the settings on the microwave.

The fairy rolled her eyes. "Trust me. Now look here. These are rings fit for a Perkins witch. Rubies as red as the luscious blood that flows through her body? Emerald as green as the grass that will one day grow over her grave? Onyx as black as the darkness of ashes after a cremation?"

The fairy really needed to work on her salesmanship. I get that she was trying to appeal to the reaper in me, but surely, she should have realized that I wasn't eagerly considering the mortality of the witch fate had chosen as my beloved. I was about to make some vague complimentary statements about the rings and head over to the firehouse when something caught my eye—a pale metal band of entwined ivy.

"Platinum. Purity and strength," the fairy murmured, pulling the ring from the case and putting it in my palm.

I ran my fingers over the tiny leaves, admiring the intricate detail, then I handed it back to the fairy.

"I'm assuming reapers don't carry cash?" She raised her eyebrows. "Visa? Debit card? Apple Pay?"

Maybe someday I'd buy this ring and give it to Ophelia, but even a reaper who'd only been in this life for less than two days knew it was too soon.

"I'm afraid I don't have any of those forms of payment.

141

Thank you for your time. You have beautiful jewelry," I told the fairy, turning to leave.

As I headed down to the firehouse, I thought about the ring. Was that really what mortals did when they loved someone? Purchase a piece of wearable art to symbolize their emotional attachment? I headed through the open bay door and past the ladder truck to where Skip sat on a plastic lawn chair that looked too flimsy to hold the weight of a giant. Next to him on another lawn chair sat a gargoyle who I assumed must be Edward.

"Should I buy Ophelia a ring?" I asked the giant.

Skip elbowed the gargoyle. "Holy crap. It's been what? Two days? And he's already wanting to buy her a ring. I thought those demons moved fast, but they've got nothing on reapers."

"I guess when you see people die all day every day, you don't sit on your thumbs and wait for the right time." The gargoyle put out his hand. "I'm Edward."

"Nash." I shook his hand, noting the granite texture of his skin and the man's crushingly firm grip.

"Hey, Flora," Skip shouted toward the back of the firehouse. "Nash wants to know if he should buy Ophelia a ring."

The Valkyrie poked her head around the doorjamb and eyed me from top to toe. "No."

She vanished while the other two laughed.

"Give it a few months, bud," Edward told me. "You don't want to scare her off."

"Think you're heading down the right path though." Skip nodded. "She seemed pretty happy with you a few nights ago."

"You hurt Ophelia, and we'll shove your scythe up your ass!" Flora shouted from the back room.

The guys laughed again. Valkyries. I hadn't come across them a whole lot as a reaper, but I knew they were violent, and I knew when they issued a threat, they meant it. I got the impression that the rest of Ophelia's co-workers felt the same. They were a close-knit bunch, and I loved that she had friends who cared so much about her.

"So, you're on a shopping trip today?" Edward nodded to the bag I carried that held my shirts and pants.

"I'm actually applying for jobs but needed to pick up a few things." I shifted the bag to my other hand. "Hopefully by the end of the week I'll be working at either the diner or the hotel."

Edward nodded thoughtfully. "Hollister's a pretty chill guy. The diner would be more hectic, but the staff there is a lot of fun. My sister used to waitress there on weekends."

"You should talk to Sheriff Oakes," Skip said. "He might want another deputy, and no one's gonna mess with a reaper. We've got our own version of the academy here, so you wouldn't have to deal with going out into the human world to train."

Given that he was the second one to mention that, I took it for a sign. When Ophelia got back, I'd run it by her. I'd definitely take the diner or the housekeeping job if offered, but it would be good to be open to other options.

"Well, I'm thinking of heading over to the hospital," I told them. "If Ophelia shows up here and I'm not back, can you send her over?"

"Absolutely." Edward stood and smacked me on the shoulder. Both men said their goodbyes, and Flora shouted a farewell from the back room as I left and walked through town to the big gray blocky building that served as Accident's hospital.

I wasn't going to see that nice nurse who was more than happy to demonstrate all the medical equipment to me, nor to reap souls, although I could tell there were a few in the hospital that would probably be getting a visit from a reaper sooner rather than later. I wanted to visit Ophelia's twin sister, Sylvie.

The guard who'd caught Ophelia and I making out in the parking lot was there at the door, giving me a nod and a knowing wink as he waved me inside. With a quick check to make sure Sylvie hadn't yet left the hospital, I headed upstairs to find her alone in her room.

Standing in the doorway, we stared at each other for a moment.

"I know you." Her voice trembled. "Are you here...for me?"

"No," I reassured her. "Ophelia made a deal and I resurrected you."

Tears sprang to her eyes. "Don't take her. Please don't take her. I can't let her die in my place."

"She's not going to die in your place." I walked in and stood beside Sylvie's bed. "I'm the one who died. I'm not a reaper any more. At least I don't *think* I'm a reaper any more. Plants. Maybe small animals. Actually, I think I *might* be able to reap a soul if I'm in the right place at the right time, but I'm not hearing the call any more. I'm not being sent all over the world to ease mortals in their transition."

"Why? Why would you do that? Why did you spare me?" she asked, her eyes searching mine.

"Because I love your sister." Love. Two years ago, I hadn't even known what that word meant, what it felt like. And now I was completely certain that Ophelia had my heart.

Sylvie's lips trembled into a smile, then she laughed. "Seriously? A reaper falls in love with my sister who is terrified of death."

"Opposites attract?" I smiled in return, pulled a chair up beside Sylvie's bed and sat. "How are you feeling today?"

"Like I was electrocuted, died, and then was forced to drink a gallon of rotted seaweed-flavored sewage," she shot back. "Actually, I don't feel bad. Glenda's smoothies make me want to puke, but they're definitely powerful potions. My chest doesn't hurt any more. My arms and legs aren't shaking any more. I'm thinking clearer. I'm remembering more about that night."

"You had memory loss?" I asked.

She nodded. "Some of that night was kind of blurry. Were we eating lasagna or ziti? Was Aaron there or not? I remembered needing to microwave the hot fudge, but nothing about what happened once I went into the kitchen. I was dead—definitely dead. I remember…I remember seeing you. I knew you were a reaper, and I felt okay about it. Not happy. Not sad. Just sort of resigned. Then there was all this pain and I was gasping for breath on the kitchen floor." She reached out and touched my arm. "You resurrected me?"

"Your soul had separated. You're right. You were dead. A life for a life." I struggled to find a way to explain it, thinking of all the books, magazine articles, and canned food labels I'd read, along with all the late-night television I'd binged on. "Without a reaper to cut the cord, you were dead, but you still remained tethered to your body. Once Ophelia acknowledged my offer and accepted it, I died in your place."

Her hand gripped my arm. "But you're still alive. And from what you said, you're still kind of a reaper."

"Death isn't final; it's just a transition," I told her. "I died as a reaper and have transformed into something else. I'm still trying to figure out what that something else is."

"And you love my sister," she prompted.

"Ophelia is my life." I thought of one of those late-night movies I'd watched. "In a wholesome, non-threatening, respectful of her autonomy sort of way."

Sylvie laughed. "Wholesome. Let me tell you right now… whatever your name is, my sister isn't as wholesome as she pretends to be. I hope your love for her includes getting busy

145

DEBRA DUNBAR

between the sheets because she could seriously use some good sex in her life."

"We've made love many times," I told her. "I'm enjoying that level of intimacy with your sister and I hope we continue to do that a lot. Several times a day."

For some reason that made Sylvie laugh so hard I thought I might need to call the doctor in.

"I *like* you, reaper. Honesty and clear communication are an essential component to any healthy relationship. So, what's your name?"

"Ophelia calls me Nash," I said.

"Nash." She nodded as if she approved. "Here's the deal, Nash who used to be a reaper and still might be when it comes to plants. Support Ophelia in everything she does because she needs someone to do that. Tell her how smart and awesome she is on a regular basis. She *is* smart and awesome, but it's always good to be adored and be adored for more than your boobs or epic blow job ability. With me so far?"

I nodded, even though I was so not with her.

"Hold her when she wakes up with nightmares and visions. Listen to her without judgement. Let her know you'll never leave her, that she'll never wake up one morning and find you gone, because that's a big fear of hers." Sylvie's voice broke a bit on that one. "It's a big fear with all of us."

"I won't leave her," I assured the witch. "Unless she tells me I need to leave, then I'll stand outside and watch and wait because she might change her mind. Is that crossing a line?"

Her lips twitched. "She'll tell you if it's crossing a line. Otherwise go with it. As for sex, you should take charge, which I understand might be hard for you since I doubt reapers did much in the boom-chicka-wow-wow depart-ment. Pay attention, and if she's reacting enthusiastically to something you're doing, then you're on the right track."

146

"Did I mention I watched a lot of adult television the other night?" I asked.

Sylvie rolled her eyes. "Go with your instincts before you start recreating porno movies. That stuff is all fake. Take your time. Pay attention to what her body is telling you."

I stood. "Thank you so much for these pointers."

"Always go with your instincts. If you feel like you should kiss her, kiss her. If you feel like you should do more than kiss her, then do more. And if she says stop, you need to stop right then and there and not proceed until she tells you otherwise. Got it?"

"Got it." I reached out to shake Sylvie's hand, then bent down and kissed her on the cheek. "Thank you. And I hope you make a full recovery soon."

"I hope so too, because Cassie is going to take me to her house and make me stay on her sofa until she's convinced I'm okay. I might need to organize a jail break." She waved me off. "Now get out of here before she comes back and wants to know who you are and why you're hanging out in my hospital room."

I fled, realizing that Ophelia's older sister wasn't someone I wanted interrogating me. On my way down the hall, I waved at the nurse from the night before, then hesitated in the elevator, hitting the button for the basement. While I was here, I might as well visit the morgue, just in case there were any souls of the departed who might need my assistance.

There was no one down the hallway or in the morgue—well, no one except a short, curvy, blonde werewolf. Everyone employed by the hospital seemed to have uniforms with bright colored pants and shirts paired with jackets with plenty of pockets. This werewolf was wearing a pair of dark jeans and a black tank top. Perhaps the morgue had a different dress code?

The werewolf didn't appear to be working. All the bodies

were stored out of sight and she was lingering over by a shiny metal table, fidgeting with a silver bowl. I was happy to realize that all their souls had departed and was about to leave when she turned to me. Her eyes widened and her nostrils flared.

"You…are you here to kill me? Your smell…you smell like death."

She was the second person to make that comment since I'd "died." Since neither Ophelia nor her sister had mentioned any strange odor, I was going to assume it was just a werewolf thing.

"I'm Nash. A reaper. Well, sort of a reaper. A retired reaper?" I walked forward and held out my hand.

She backed up, holding the bowl in front of her.

"Did Dallas send you?" There was a strangely hopeful note in her voice.

"No. I just came down to see if the dead needed any help."

"Good." She stamped her foot, gripping the silver bowl tightly. "Because if he wants me back, then he needs to come himself and not send some death-smelling lackey. Actually, he shouldn't bother because I'm not coming back. Or maybe I'm coming back, but I'm not going to mate with him. He's a pig and I changed my mind."

I stared at her. "Okay."

She put down the bowl and started to pace the room. "I figured I could hide here, that being underground with all these refrigeration units and dead people might make it harder for him to track me down. Are they looking for me? The other werewolves? Did you see them looking for me?"

"No." I had no idea what this woman was talking about. "Do you want them to be looking for you?"

"No! He'll kill me if he finds me. Make me go through with the mating ceremony or kill me. I've humiliated him and he'll kill me. Or my mother will kill me. Or I'll be exiled and have to live in this town for the rest of my life, so I might as well die."

"Um, is there something I could do to help you?" Ophelia had said she was going up to the werewolf compound to talk to them about a personal matter. I was beginning to put the puzzle pieces together and get the idea that whatever was going on, this woman was in the middle of it all.

"Don't tell anyone I'm here," she urged. "Forget you saw me. If they know, my life will be in danger."

"I have to tell Ophelia," I told her because I couldn't promise to keep her secret, not from the one woman who I needed to be completely honest with.

"No!" She ran toward me and grabbed my arm. "You can't tell any of the witches. They'll storm up there and get in Dallas' face and I'll end up exiled. I don't know what I want to do yet. I know I don't want to go through with the mating ceremony, but I don't like the idea of living my life as a lone wolf. Promise me you won't tell anyone."

"I promise." The lie came far easier than I'd ever thought it would. "You stay here and hide. I'll keep your secret and make sure you're safe."

With that, I left and headed back over to the firehouse, determined to tell Ophelia the moment she returned from the werewolf compound.

CHAPTER 15

I made a quick call to Bronwyn on my way to Shelby and Alberta's, just to see if anyone had gone across the wards. Few things would cause a disruption in the wards, and Bronwyn was particularly susceptible to a break in our perimeters, but I wasn't sure if her witchy senses tingled when folks came and went or not.

"You've got to be joking me," she said. "Do you know how annoying that would be? Every time someone ran out to the mall, or your crew responded to an accident on the highway, or the wolves chased a deer past the wards? It would be like a non-stop buzzing in my head."

"People don't cross the wards that often," I corrected her. Bronwyn was prone to exaggeration. Normally it was cute, but not today.

"There's nothing forbidding anyone from leaving the town," she reminded me. "But I doubt she left. Remember the risk residents take when they live outside the wards. If this werewolf was fleeing a mating, she'd be better off running to Cassie for sanctuary in the town. She's safer in Accident than trying to live as a lone wolf outside the wards."

Bronwyn was right. Outside, Tink would risk exposure to humans as well as other werewolf packs. "So, she's probably still within the wards."

"She's probably still within the compound. Or, at the very least, on the mountain. There are plenty of places up there for her to hide, and I'm sure she's got friends in the pack that would be sympathetic. Not everyone who accepts Dallas as the alpha is on board with everything he says and does."

"But they could track her," I countered. "If she was on the mountain, why wouldn't Dallas just sniff her out? Or her mother? Actually, why didn't her mother go furry and track her down before going to Dallas and admitting her daughter bolted?"

Bronwyn snorted. "Hell, if I know. Maybe Dallas is reluctant to go drag a woman home by her hair like some Neanderthal. Wouldn't be good for his image to look like he had to force a female to mate with him. It's probably better for him to act like nothing's wrong and he's not bothered, like she's just off hunting or at a spa weekend or her bachelorette party."

I pulled off the road just before the bridge and parked, thinking to myself that Bronwyn was probably right.

"Hey, I'll call you back later," I told her as I got out of my car and headed down the dirt path that led under the bridge and to the tiny house Shelby shared with Alberta.

Shelby answered the door and ushered me inside. Alberta was cutting onions and turnips in the kitchenette. The three of us filled the small house. I sat, feeling claustrophobic, my eyes watering from the onion aroma.

"Did you find her?" Shelby asked, twisting her hands together. "Is she okay?"

"She's welcome to stay here if she needs to," Alberta chimed in. "We've got plenty of room."

They didn't, but I got the idea that in troll terms, Alberta's house was McMansion sized.

"Do you have any idea who Tink's mom wanted her to marry?" I asked Shelby. "Who is the suitor?"

"She didn't tell me."

"I think it's Dallas." I explained all the reasons why I thought that as well as the results of my visit to Dallas and to Clinton.

"It makes sense," Shelby said. "Except most female were-wolves would be honored and delighted to mate with Dallas."

"Would you?" I asked.

"Uh, no. But I'm in love with someone else," Shelby said with a quick smile behind her at Alberta. "Before I fell in love, I...well, I probably wouldn't have been *thrilled* to marry Dallas, but it would have been a good career move, so to speak. Mate to the pack alpha? Instant respect and obedience, plus just about anything my heart desired."

"Except for a faithful spouse," I countered.

She grimaced. "That, and Dallas can be a bit of an ass. Jump when he says jump. Do whatever he wants without hesitation. That sort of thing. He's not someone you want to anger, so his mate can forget about ever asserting her opinion on anything or standing up to him if she disagrees. It would be a life of submissive agreement, although I guess she could take out her frustrations on the other wolves in the pack."

"Until they complain enough to Dallas that he decides he needs to set his mate straight," Alberta commented. "You would have lasted five seconds as his mate, my feisty wolf-girl."

I grimaced, realizing that I needed to finish up this visit because I got the idea there was going to be some sex going on here real soon, and that wasn't something I wanted to see.

"Where would Tink have gone?" I asked. "I'm worried

about her—more worried than I was when you came to see me at the diner. She's been gone since last night."

"Ruby and Dallas probably aren't going to hunt for her unless she's gone long enough to raise suspicions about his prowess as a lady killer." Shelby shrugged. "I'm assuming she's safe for now, and that she'll come to me or Cassie if she needs help. I was worried her mother had her locked away but sounds like she's run off and found someone to help her."

Alberta walked over and wrapped an arm around Shelby's shoulder. "Dinner's almost ready. We've got a few moments if you'd like to..."

And I was out of there. "Let me know if you hear anything from Tink," I told Shelby as I headed for the door. She didn't answer me as she was now lip-locked with her troll. I was just happy that I'd gotten out of the house just in time.

The werewolf thing was a bust. It probably had nothing to do with my visions in spite of what I'd told Dallas and Clinton. Tink was most likely holed up in a friend's spare room. I still had the rest of the day free and I intended to use it to check in on my sister, then to spend the remaining daylight hours getting to know Nash better.

And after the sun set? I thought of Alberta and Shelby locked in a passionate embrace and decided that maybe, just maybe, my evening would include some lovemaking of my own.

CHAPTER 16

OPHELIA

I'd caught Sylvie just as she was checking out and Cassie was getting ready to wheel her down to the car. My twin had one of Glenda's smoothies in one hand and an elephant plushie in the other. We paused to talk for a few minutes, then I let her go with a promise to come see her tomorrow. Cassie would fuss over her for the next few weeks before allowing her to go home to her own apartment, and I was sure with all the coddling she could use visitors.

One thing Sylvie had told me before I'd left that had me smiling the whole way over to the firehouse was that Nash had come to the hospital to see her. On his own, he'd taken the initiative to check in on my sister. That in my mind pretty much made him family right there.

When I got to the firehouse, the scene there further warmed my heart. Nash was being shown all the gear and equipment on the pumper truck, a fireman's hat perched on his head.

"How do I look?" He grinned over at me.

"Not sure having a reaper as a first responder is such a great idea. Maybe you should think about another career."

"Hey, Pierre is a vampire. If citizens can deal with a vampire providing medical care, then they should have no problems with me hauling them out of burning buildings."

The people inside of Accident didn't have a problem with Fernando or any of the vampires, and the people outside of Accident had no idea their paramedic was anything other than a somewhat pale human, so maybe he was right.

Nash took off the helmet, handing it over to Ricky. "I think I'll explore other options before making a decision on my life's career, though."

"We'd still welcome you as a volunteer," Ricky told him before turning to me. "Did you know your boyfriend is fireproof?"

Boyfriend. Yes, my heart was toasty warm right now.

Fireproof?

"Watch this." Ricky pulled a lighter out of his pocket and grabbed a flyer for Uptown Bakery off a nearby table. Then in violation of firehouse policy, he set the brochure on fire.

Nash reached out and took it from him, his hands passing through the flames. Then he crumpled the brochure, smothering the fire with his palms. Once done, he dusted the soot and charred paper from his hands and held his palms up to me. They were dirty, but the skin wasn't even blistered.

"Nice trick," I told him. "If you're not interested in a volunteer job at the firehouse, then I suggest you go into performance magic."

"I'll add it to my list." He picked up a shopping bag and wrapped an arm around my waist, kissing me on my temple. "Ready to go?"

We strolled down the street, and at my car, Nash put out a hand to stop me. "I've got something I need to tell you. I was asked to keep this a secret, but I shouldn't keep secrets from you."

I was liking this man more and more. "Okay. What is it?"

"I met a werewolf in the hospital—a female werewolf. She's hiding down in the morgue."

No! It couldn't be. Although the morgue was an excellent place to hide. The thick walls, the refrigeration units, the smell of decay, although faint, would smell strong to a were-wolf nose—all that would mask Tink's scent from anyone trying to find her. And who in the world would look for a werewolf in the morgue? The only people who willingly went there besides the employees were ghouls. Actually, we had to ward that section of the hospital *against* ghouls because nobody wanted to show up to claim Great Uncle Ralph only to find that a ghoul had stolen his limbs and turned them into a lovely Bolognese sauce.

Which brought up another issue. "Why were you in the morgue?"

Nash held up his hands. "I didn't kill anyone, I swear. I was visiting your sister, and thought I'd go down to make sure no souls were un-reaped. I honestly thought she worked there until she started ranting about someone trying to force her into marriage and how she was worried she'd be tracked down and killed."

I nodded. "I believe you. And I'm thrilled that I know where Tink is hiding out. She's safe? She's not hurt or in need of immediate help or anything, is she?"

"No, she's fine. She seems…agitated. I think that's the right word. Annoyed. Do you want to go speak to her?"

I thought about that for a moment. Really, I only wanted to know she was safe. "Maybe tomorrow morning. I'm thinking I should give her the night to think about every-thing and decide what she wants to do."

But would she be safe? There were employees who came and went in the morgue, and Tink might not be able to hide from them. Would they tell the pack? Kick her out? Turn her over to Dallas or one of his wolves? I really didn't want to push her to make a decision before she was ready, but I wanted to make sure she wasn't attacked in the night.

So I made a phone call.

And when I was done, I turned to Nash with a smile. "You've explored the town. Let me show you my favorite part of Accident—not the city itself, but the eastern side where I live."

"I've seen your house already. Not that I'm not thrilled to be going back there," he said with a smile.

"Not my house. I want to show you the marshes and how pretty it all is, especially at sunset."

We went over to Matilda's Good Eats and got an enormous quantity of take-out food including pan-fried chicken, black-eyed-pea salad, raspberry cobbler, and some buttermilk biscuits that she'd just taken out of the oven. Then we ran across the street and got a bottle of wine along with two plastic wine glasses and a cheap corkscrew.

Driving east, we parked at my house, then walked toward the marshes. Nash helped me carry it all to a solid strip of ground and spread the blanket while I pulled our food from the bags. It wasn't fancy with paper napkins, plastic silverware, and Styrofoam containers, but I wasn't a fancy sort of woman.

Nash sat down beside me, and we ate, enjoying the food and wine and watching as all the locals that called the marsh their home frolicked in the water. A few mermaids stopped by to join us, then a sprite, then a couple of undine and a nymph. Before long, we had half the neighborhood picnicking with us, bringing their own food and drink as well as lawn chairs and blankets. We all watched the sun set over the marshes, then Nash and I gathered up our belongings and walked back to the house.

I took my cell phone out to light the path between the houses and saw that there was a text message.

"Hey, you got a job offer from the diner," I told Nash. "If you want, you can start Thursday morning."

"I think I'd like that better than the cleaning job." The reaper looked up at the sky, his face thoughtful. "Both the fairy at the jewelry store and your co-workers at the fire-house thought I should reach out to your sheriff for job opportunities."

"That's a good idea." I stopped at the front door and turned to him, trying to read his expression in the dim light. "What *do* you want out of this new life, Nash? I know you probably haven't been here long enough to truly figure that out, but is there something you always wanted to experience as a reaper?"

He smiled and reached out to touch my hair. "Yes, and I have experienced it."

"Besides us," I said. "I realize most of your contact with mortals is during a fatality, but maybe something caught your eye? Something that seemed fun that you'd wished you could do?"

"Like ride a motorcycle? Or pet a kitten?"

"We'll make a list," I told him. "Like with the job search." This would be fun. A bucket list of things to do now that he was a retired reaper.

He nodded. "And I'd like to play a video game. And mow the grass. And grow rosebushes."

I grimaced. "That last one might be kind of tough."

He laughed. "Okay, kill some rosebushes. How about that? And…and I want to have a party."

My eyebrows shot up. "A party?"

"I went to a lot of parties as a reaper and they always looked like such fun—until someone died, that is."

"Okay, a party where no one dies." I thought for a second about that. "Lots of parties. We'll organize a neighborhood cookout here—that will be fun. And I'll take you to Pistol

Pete's when he's got a band playing—that's pretty much like a giant party. And you'll be coming to Sunday night dinners with my family at Cassie's house, of course."

His eyes searched mine. "Is that what you were doing when your sister…."

I nodded. "Sylvie likes you. I can't wait for you to meet my other sisters, and the demons, and my cousin Aaron. We get together every Sunday night. Just family."

"Family?"

His expression was so hopeful, so tentative, as if he couldn't believe how lucky he was. My heart warmed because I knew how he felt.

"Yes, family. And that now includes you."

CHAPTER 17

OPHELIA

*S*adly, there was not time for even a quickie the next morning. We both showered, ate toast, and drank coffee, and we were out the door and on our way into town. Taking the elevator down to the basement level of the hospital, I saw Babylon standing outside the door to the morgue, keeping watch.

She yawned when she saw me. "Please tell me you brought coffee? The stuff they have here sucks giant donkey balls."

"You left her alone to go get coffee?" Clearly nothing had happened last night, but I still was a bit irritated that Lonnie could have been so lax in her guard duties.

My sister rolled her eyes. "No, dufus. Of course I didn't. I sent one of the dead guys upstairs to get coffee for me. If I'm going to hang out in a morgue all night, might as well make use of the residents."

"Sorry." I grimaced, thinking again that Lonnie's magic was pretty creepy stuff. "Lonnie, this is Nash. Nash, my youngest sister Lonnie."

"So, you're dating the reaper now?" Babylon eyed Nash. "Sylvie didn't die, so I'm giving this relationship my tentative approval."

"Thanks," I drawled. "How is Tink doing?"

"Welp, she spent the night in a room full of stainless steel and dead dudes, so there's that. Actually, I think she was fine until I animated my coffee-delivery guy. That's when she told me I had to stay out here in the hall and not do any more magic."

I was pretty sure Tink would have changed her mind if Dallas and his crew had shown up to get her. Nothing scares werewolves more than an undead army.

"I appreciate the help," I told my sister. "Go on home and get some sleep. Nash and I will take it from here."

Lonnie saluted, then smiled. "Thanks for calling me, Ophelia. Thanks for letting me help and not treating me like I'm a baby, or like my magic is too icky to be useful."

"It's because your magic *is* icky that it's useful," I teased her.

She walked off, giving me the finger behind her back. I chuckled, then followed Nash into the morgue.

It was a good thing he'd gone in first because something that looked like a bedpan bounced off his shoulder.

"You jerk! I told you it was a secret and next thing I know some freaky witch shows up to 'guard' me. She's a necromancer. Do you know how horrible it is to be stuck in a morgue all night with a necromancer?"

Nash batted a trashcan away and stood in front of me. I leaned around his shoulder to see Tink over by one of the tables, an assortment of projectiles at hand.

"Do you really think Dallas couldn't sniff you out if he wanted to?" I asked her. "I spoke with him yesterday. Both he and your mother were just biding their time, waiting for you

161

to return. How long before he decides you've humiliated him enough and he comes to drag you back home? You should thank Nash for telling me so I could provide not just for your safety, but for the safety of everyone here in the hospital."

She hesitated, a metal tray in her hand. "I didn't...I didn't think about that. I don't want anyone here to get hurt."

I gave Nash's shoulder a shove, but he refused to budge. "I hate to push you to make a decision, Tink, but I need to know. Are you going to go back to the compound and willingly go through with the mating ceremony, or do you want us to provide you with sanctuary?"

She set the tray down and ran a hand over her face. "I don't want to be an outcast. I don't want to be exiled and have no one ever talk to me again—although right now I might be happy if my *mother* never talked to me again. I can't believe she took his side over mine. What mother does that?"

I grimaced, thinking that Tink might not want to blame her mother too much. Dallas *was* pack alpha, after all. Although I couldn't imagine not supporting my daughter in something like this.

"Is there any way you can get out of the engagement?" I asked her, still peering around Nash's shoulder. The guy would not move, even though Tink had put down her weapons.

The werewolf sniffed, wiping her eyes. "No. I mean, not unless Dallas agrees to it. And he won't. Mom already told a few people, and it's gonna make him look like a fool if I back out. Dallas hates looking like a fool."

"What if he tells everyone that it was his idea to back out?" I asked. "He can make you look like a fool instead."

Tink's eyes sparked with anger and for a second, I thought she was going to pick up the tray again. "I'm not a fool!" she snapped.

"Maybe Dallas can let everyone know he found a female werewolf he likes better and that he'd dumped you for her."

"That better not happen," she snarled.

These werewolf egos were driving me nuts. "How about if we make your mom out to be the idiot instead? Dallas can say he was thinking of you as a possible mate, but nothing had been decided yet, and Ruby jumped the gun on it all."

Tink let out a breath. "Okay. That sounds good. I just want to go back and live in the compound, but not marry that skank of werewolf. And not have it look like he jilted me for someone else."

"Got it." I didn't have it, but I figured it was best to just wing it and do the best I could. "Come with us," I told Tink. "I'm going to take you over to Cassie's house where you can get something to eat, sleep in a decent bed, and have a demon watch over you. Nash and I will go talk to Dallas and see what we can do."

I wasn't sure how well that conversation was going to go. Having Nash along would help, even though all he seemed to be able to do was kill plants. I looped my arm through his as we headed out of the hospital, thinking that it might be a good idea to make a quick stop on our way up to the were-wolf compound—to the one sister who might have something I could actually use as a weapon.

* * *

"I NEED A WEAPON." Bronwyn and I stood in her work-shop/garage while Nash sat out on the porch with Hadur drinking a beer. "I need something that I can use against a werewolf, not to kill him or anything, but to knock him down or render him unconscious or something."

It truly sucked that I was the only one of the Perkins witches that didn't have any defensive capabilities. Cassie's go-to was fire. Bronwyn enchanted objects that could drop a dragon at fifty feet. Sylvie was a luck witch but could also hex and even curse, although she didn't want anyone knowing about that. Adrienne could raise an attack army of wasps with a snap of her fingers. Babylon could raise an attack army of undead with a snap of her fingers.

I was an oracle. And throwing prophecies at someone wasn't exactly a good defense mechanism. Dallas was hardly going to back off because I told him he'd leave the window on his truck open during the storm next Tuesday and his upholstery would be soaked.

Lame. So very lame.

Bronwyn wrinkled her nose. "I don't have much handy right now. I've been so busy with farrier work, and…. well, with Hadur."

I hid a grin, thrilled that my sister had found love. "A spare towel? Like what you did for Pistol Pete's?"

"Hardly. That took forever to make. Metal is easier for me to enchant," she said.

Pete's towel was legendary. It was Bronwyn's magnum opus, although she'd produced some other pretty spectacular objects as well.

"Spoons like you did in the cabin?" I suggested.

"I could have half a dozen done by tomorrow night," she said. "I need Hadur to help me, otherwise it would take me until next week to pull that together. I'm sorry, Ophelia. I just can't do a lot of magic on the spot like Cassie can."

And Cassie wasn't any good at enchanting objects. For her to help, I'd need to actually bring her with me, and I didn't feel like pouring gasoline on the fire between her and the pack right now.

"How about your nippers?" I asked, thinking of the farrier tool Bronwyn had enchanted. "Can I borrow your nippers?"

"No, you most certainly cannot borrow my favorite pair

of nippers." She glared at me. "Besides, the enchantment on those wore off weeks ago. I've only got one item I was working on that's finished and I don't see how it would be of much help."

"I'll take it." Whatever it was, it was better than nothing. Although after I'd said the words, I did wonder what sort of weirdness I'd be possibly using as a weapon against Dallas. Windchimes that chimed without any wind? A fireplace poker that absorbed stray sparks? A hammer that shrank down to pocket-size when not in use? Bronwyn made some pretty quirky stuff.

"I made it for Marcus. He's gonna be really pissed off if I let you have it and you break it," she warned. "And I won't take the heat for it, either. You break it, you deal with the angry panther shifter."

Crap, what was this thing? I immediately thought of all sorts of weird metal sex toys that Bronwyn might enchant for a horny panther shifter. Having Sylvie for a sister, I knew about spreader bars, love-cuffs, sex swings and the like. Who knew what Marcus had paid Bronwyn to work her magic on?

I swallowed hard, not wanting to have to defend myself with an eighteen-inch magicked metal dildo. Although it would probably be effective. I couldn't imagine Dallas being more afraid of anything than a witch running at him with an enchanted Ass-Pounder 3000.

"Okay. I'll take it. And I'll be the one facing the firing squad if I break Marcus' toy."

Bronwyn went into the back of her garage and came out with a three-foot length of metal. It wasn't an Ass-Pounder 3000. It was a golf club—a nine iron, to be precise.

"Marcus golfs?" I was completely shocked at the idea of the sexy panther shifter taking to the fairway. Although I probably shouldn't have been. Lawyers golfed, didn't they?

Well, except for Cassie. Men lawyers golfed—at least that was the stereotype running through my head. I just couldn't imagine Marcus in plaid pants, driving a cart down a path through manicured greens and shooting par.

Although he probably *didn't* shoot par, which would be the reason he'd left his nine iron here with Bronwyn to enchant.

"Please tell me it's magicked to beat supernatural creatures to a pulp," I pleaded.

Bronwyn shook her head. "Nope. You'll hit straight and far every time. No slice. No hook. No duffing. Swing, and that ball will fly like you were Tiger Woods."

I barely knew who Tiger Woods was, and I had no idea what slicing, hooking, or duffing meant, but it was the only option. I took the club from my sister, interested to note that it was lightweight and well balanced. Marcus had clearly spent a lot on this thing even pre-enchantment.

"Got any golf balls to go with it?" The vision suddenly returned. Golf balls. It was too weird a coincidence not to ignore. The vision had included golf balls, so clearly this club had something to do with what would happen. Something dead in the woods. Blood on leaves. Moon on the mountain. Blood leading to Shelby's front door.

And golf balls.

Bronwyn headed back into the garage and came out with a purple felt bag that at one time held Crown Royal. She handed it to me, and I opened it, finding about ten golf balls inside.

"I've just gotta ask why you've got these, and why they're in a whisky bag?"

She shrugged. "I did some work on the safety cage at Butler Ridge Driving Range, and they gave them to me along with a gift card for their putting course."

"And you kept them."

"You know me. I never throw anything away." She grinned. "And now you have a really sweet pro-level PGA tour-type nine iron and a bunch of golf balls. Go play eighteen holes or whack Dallas over the head with it or whatever. Your call."

CHAPTER 18

OPHELIA

*N*ash and I stood in the same room where I'd met Dallas before, except this time there were no offers of booze or other beverages. The werewolf who'd escorted us in had left us to wait, giving my golf club a puzzled glance and evidently deciding to not consider it a weapon. He had been a bit nervous about Nash, his nostrils flaring as he took in the reaper's odd scent, but neither my companion nor my nine iron evidently warranted questions.

When Dallas arrived, this time he was accompanied by a short stocky female werewolf with light brown hair and a healthy amount of golden fuzz on her chin and jaw line. Her eyes were sharp as she took me in, hesitating on the nine iron and widening as she saw Nash.

Dallas stopped abruptly just past the doorway, also staring at Nash. "You smell... you smell like death."

"Well, that's not very nice," I chided. "There's no need to comment about someone's personal hygiene."

"I don't mean death as in decaying flesh. I mean death." Dallas scowled at Nash. "What *are* you?"

"A reaper."

168

Nash said it with all the cheerfulness of someone announcing free ice cream sundaes. What made it even more amusing was Ruby and Dallas' reaction.

"Who's going to die?" Dallas asked through clenched teeth.

"Everyone eventually." Nash smiled. "Hopefully no one today. That all depends on you, though."

Dallas sucked in a breath and Ruby took a step backward while I shot Nash a grateful glance. As far as we knew, he couldn't reap more than plants, and he'd never had the ability to kill someone indiscriminately, but the threat would ensure Dallas and Ruby would behave. And if they didn't…well, I had a golf club and a pocket full of balls.

I got right to the point. "Tink is in town, and she's not coming back unless you break off the mating."

Dallas eyed Nash, then turned to me. "This is ridiculous. She agreed to the mating. She's already pledged, given her word. It's a done deal and the ceremony is a mere formality. She needs to get her butt back here and honor her commitment."

"What's joined cannot be separated," Ruby added. "Mating is for life. It's our pack law. It's our culture. This isn't a single werewolf deciding to break their pack bonds and live as a lone wolf. She's pledged. And a mate has every right to insist his mate return to his side. Even a Perkins witch can't force a mated pair apart."

"But you're *not* mated," I told Dallas. "And there are cases of divorce among werewolves. You don't really want an unwilling bride, do you? You must realize how miserable she could make your life if you force her."

"I'm the alpha," Dallas blustered.

"Even alphas sleep sometimes," Nash added.

Dallas snarled, and I held out my hands to pacify him. "I'm not saying violence. It's the little things. Toenails painted bright red while you sleep. Hair removal cream in your bath wash. Every meal she cooks for you is overdone or your least favorite item. Clothing ruined in the laundry. Favorite items accidently broken. Rumors that you can't perform in bed or that you've got a little dick. Trust me, Dallas, you do not want an unwilling woman for your mate."

The alpha began to pace, keeping his eye on Nash the whole time. "She'll rue the day she does any of that. I'm not letting her back out now. It's too late. Her refusing to return and go through with the ceremony would be an unforgivably humiliating slight on me as the leader of this pack. First my own son defies me and fractures my pack without even issuing a challenge and now this? No. Just...no."

Crap, this wasn't going well. I eyed my golf club and wondered if it would be possible for me to knock some sense into the werewolf.

"Find a way to save face, then. Her mother jumped the gun and spread the news before you'd decided whether or not to offer for Tink. Yes, you considered it, but you've decided not to go through with it. Make up some excuse, like she's not pretty enough or is a crappy cook, or doesn't want pups, or shaves her legs. Make something up, cancel the mating ceremony, and let her come back to the pack as a single werewolf."

Tink was going to be furious about this. Her ego was just as big as Dallas' and she'd have a fit about being dumped. Too bad. Screw her pride. If Tink wanted to come back to the pack badly enough, then she'd have to suck it up and deal with a little humiliation. After all, she was the one going back on her promise here, and it probably was too much to ask for Dallas to look the chump in this whole thing.

"This is stupid," Ruby snapped. "If she's not back by night-fall, I'll sniff her out and drag her home myself."

Nash stiffened beside me and I reached out to touch his

arm. We didn't need this to get physical, and at the end of the day, it was Dallas' decision that would be the important one, not Ruby's.

"I'll break off the mating," Dallas finally said. "She's crazy and a crappy cook and can't hunt worth shit. And she shaves her legs. I'll let everyone know the mating was a hopeful rumor spread by Tink and her mother, and that I was *never* seriously considering her."

Ruby let out a cry and covered her mouth, then with a look from Dallas she bent her head in submission.

"There's no reason for me to ever see her again outside of pack functions," Dallas added. "Ruby will go into town at moonrise tonight to speak to Cassie about her daughter. It's between them if Tink returns to the pack or decides to be a lone wolf. It's not my business. I'll abide by whatever Cassie and Ruby agree to."

I let out a breath I hadn't realized I'd been holding. "Cassie can meet Ruby in the park across from the diner. Ruby can have two or three werewolves accompany her if she would feel safer that way, as Cassie will have Lucien by her side."

Ruby slumped but remained silent, knowing that at this point, she would have no choice but to do as Dallas said. This was the way things were in the werewolf pack.

"Agreed," Dallas said. "Ruby and two werewolves will meet Cassie in the park at moonrise, and between them they will decide if Tink returns or not."

Dallas spun about to leave the room, snapping his fingers. Ruby fell in behind him, her head still lowered. I waited until the pair had left, then raised a finger to my lips to signal to Nash that we should wait until we were out of hearing range of the werewolves before we discussed anything.

Once we were halfway down the mountain, the reaper turned to me. "So? Did that go as well as it seemed on the face of things, or were you getting the same uneasy feeling I was?"

"Same uneasy feeling," I told him. "We need to go talk to Cassie. My hope is that she'll be able to convince Ruby not to disown Tink."

"And Dallas?" Nash asked.

I looked in my rearview mirror at the winding road that led up to the pack compound. "It's possible that he meant what he said, that he'll trash Tink and claim he never wanted her to begin with."

"Or?"

"Or he digs in his heels like Dallas has done over every single thing in his life and refuses to give in. If that's the case, then I expect a whole lot more to happen at moonrise tonight than a tense discussion in a diner."

"You think while your sister and Ruby are talking, he'll sneak in and grab Tink?"

I nodded. "That's exactly what I think. And that's exactly what we need to prepare for."

* * *

"I DON'T LIKE THIS." My eldest sister scowled, crossing her arms in front of her chest. Lucien mirrored her pose, and I bit back a smile.

"I know you don't like it, but I don't trust Dallas."

"I don't trust him either, which is why I think it would be better for us to guard Tink and confront him while you both negotiate with Ruby," she told me.

"I'm not in a position to negotiate with Ruby," I pointed out. "You're the head witch. You're the muscle here. It's bad enough that Tink is going to be slandered for being a lousy cook and shaving her legs or whatever. I want to make sure she's not only allowed back into the pack, but that her mother isn't going to throw her out of the house and disown her. You're in a position to play the heavy and make sure Ruby doesn't make Tink's return any more of an issue then it's already going to be."

"I don't want you facing down Dallas." Cassie frowned. "You're an oracle. I'd rather Bronwyn meet him with Hadur at her side if it can't be me and Lucien."

"I've got the only enchanted item Bronwyn had to spare," I told her. "Actually, I'm in a better position to beat down Dallas and keep Tink safe than Bronwyn right now. And I've got Nash to help me."

They booth looked over at the reaper, who shrugged. "Evidently I smell alarming and the werewolves think I can kill them with a touch. If Dallas gets out of hand, I'll start killing off plants and wave my hands around, and he'll run for it."

"I'll even dress Nash in a robe with a scythe if that helps," I added.

Cassie sighed. "So, Lucien and I are supposed to meet Ruby in the park across from the diner? Then go into the diner for blackberry cobbler and a nice chat?"

I nodded. "I'm trying to think of the best place for us to safeguard Tink. It needs to be somewhere defensible and somewhere without a lot of others who might wind up being collateral damage if there's a fight."

"There better not be a fight," Cassie scowled. "I don't like this, Ophelia. We almost lost Sylvie this week. I don't like putting you in danger."

I was a bit offended that she was perfectly fine putting Bronwyn in danger. Although I think she was relying on Hadur to protect her if she needed assistance. The warmonger was obviously pretty darned good in a fight, and the werewolves were just as nervous around him as they were around Lucien. Or Nash.

"I'll be fine, Cassie." I held up my hand. "I promise. Now where should we keep Tink? I don't like the morgue as it would put everyone in the hospital at risk if Dallas attacked. Out at my house, maybe?"

"The park," Lucien said. "That way if there's trouble, we'll be right over at the diner and near enough to help."

"There's that open space by the fountain," Cassie added. "That way you can see any wolves coming at you from the tree line or the bushes."

Tree line. And those bushes? They were oleanders. I suddenly felt something heavy settle in my stomach. Was this the rest of my vision? Was someone going to die tonight?

I pushed away that thought because Lucien and Cassie were right. The park was an ideal spot to keep Tink safe. If Dallas attacked and Nash and I couldn't handle it, Cassie and Lucien were within shouting distance. And if Dallas didn't attack and everything went well inside the diner, then Tink could return to the mountain with her mother.

Nash reached out and put an arm around my shoulder. "It's going to be fine."

"Who's doing the divination now?" I teased as I put my arm around his waist. "Actually, I agree with you. Dallas isn't an idiot. He's not going to bring an army into Accident and risk having Cassie come burn *his* beard off as well. If he comes at all, he'll sneak in with a few wolves and try to do a quick grab. We can fend him off."

"If you need help, let us know," Cassie said.

I smiled, leaning against Nash's side. "I won't need help. I've got a reaper and an enchanted golf club."

CHAPTER 19

OPHELIA

The moon broke free from the clouds, illuminating the landscape in a rolling wave of light. During the day, the city park was a beautiful mix of tame and wild, just like the residents of our town. Wild roses and overgrown azaleas gave the park thick, thorny, private spots to enjoy. At the west end of the park, a small grove gave the illusion of a vast woods complete with mossy paths and thick undergrowth. In the center of the park was a manicured lawn, perfect for croquet or a foot—or hoof— race. In the middle was a small fountain with fresh water spilling into clean bowls positioned at different heights, providing a quick drink to those who needed it. Around the fountain and at the edge of the lawn were bushes with long, thin leaves that in daylight would be dark green.

Oleander. Oleander in the moonlight.

I saw Tink stiffen and look off into the distance, her eyes focusing on something deep in the wooded grove. Cassie lifted a hand and a ball of light appeared, fire flickering around the edges. Three werewolves walked from the tree line—Ruby flanked on either side by two heavily bearded men in camo. They hesitated as they saw my sister's ball of fiery light, then glanced over at Lucien who was now nearly seven feet tall with huge horns sprouting from his forehead and glowing orange eyes.

"Don't want any trouble," Ruby called out. "I'm just here to talk about my daughter."

Out of the corner of my eye, I saw Tink stiffen. Her mother hadn't spoken to her or even looked at her. It was as if the female werewolf wasn't even here. Dallas had said he wouldn't get involved, so it was clear Tink wouldn't be exiled or forbidden to return to the pack, but would her mother accept her again? Life in the pack would be difficult without the social status that familial bonds provided.

Cassie's ball of light vanished. "Then let's go to the diner and talk. Peach pie and coffee. I'll buy."

The two male werewolves perked up at that, and I bit back a grin. Shifters were always hungry, and everyone knew the way to a werewolf's heart was through his or her stomach—which was probably why the criticism of Tink's cooking would really sting.

We watched as the five headed into the diner. I shifted so Tink had Nash and I on either side, the fountain at our backs.

"She's gonna disown me," Tink said tearfully. "I won't have a family. I'll be stripped of my last name. Everyone will think I'm a bad cook and a leg shaver, and that Dallas not only dumped me but decided I wasn't pretty enough to even screw. Nobody will invite me to hunt with them. No one will ever date me—especially if they think I shave my legs. I'll never have sex again. I'll die a lonely wolf, shriveled up from the lack of orgasms."

I fought the urge to roll my eyes.

"I've heard that Ophelia's sister, Sylvie, has an incredible knowledge of sex toys," Nash chimed in. "There's no reason for you to die from lack of orgasms when there are any number of battery-operated products to fill your needs."

I choked, slapping a hand over my mouth.

"Those toys are not fun unless there's a virile werewolf male to enjoy them with," she complained. "I'm not a do-it-yourself woman here."

"I'm sure this will all quickly blow over and everyone will forget about it," I told her. "You'll have lots of male were-wolves propositioning you, and Dallas will find some other woman to mate with."

Tink looked oddly depressed at my statement, but before she could say another word, something caught her attention from within the grove. A tiny smile quivered at the corner of her mouth. "They're here," she whispered.

My eyes narrowed, and I wondered for a brief second what the heck was going on in that little werewolf brain of hers. Unfortunately, I didn't have time to ask, because she was right—there were werewolves in the grove, and I was darned sure one of them was Dallas.

I could hear them in the bushes, which meant they weren't exactly being stealthy in their approach. Tink caught her breath and spun around, moving in closer to the two of us.

"Protect her," I told Nash, not really sure what he would be able to do beyond kill a bunch of plants. His presence seemed to unsettle the werewolves, so my hope was they'd be afraid enough of him that they wouldn't attack.

Stepping a few feet away, I upended a box of golf balls onto the ground, noticing how much they looked like the full moon peeking over the edge of the horizon. Then I lowered the golf club, wiggled my hips, and tried to look like the golfers I'd seen on television.

"Stand back or feel the wrath of my...my nine iron," I commanded.

A wolf sprang from the bushes, and I swung. The club hit the ball with a solid thwack. The wolf yelped and scurried backward as it hit him in the chest. Two more wolves ran forward, and I drove them both back with solid blows to the side and head. The next time the three were a whole lot more cautious, and all I had to do was pretend like I was swinging to make them dodge back to safety.

A deep growl filled the air and I caught my breath as a huge dark wolf slunk forward, teeth bared, and yellow eyes fixed not on me but on Tink.

Dallas. I hit golf balls like a crazy woman. He grunted with each impact, but kept moving slowly forward like he was stalking his prey. The last golf ball bounced off his head and, out of options, I ran forward, swinging the club at him.

It seemed like the golf club wasn't just accurate when it came to hitting golf balls. The nine iron bent nearly in half as it encountered the werewolf alpha's thick skull. Blood flew from my club on the upswing, splattering the oleander leaves. Dallas' eyes rolled back in his head and he dropped like a stone, shifting back into his human form.

Behind me, I heard Tink scream and Nash shout for her to stay back. A slight female form shoved me aside, cursing as she dropped to the ground beside the naked, unconscious alpha.

Cursing. At me. As if I'd just killed her puppy and not bravely defended her from the jerk who was trying to force her into a loveless marriage.

"Is he dead? Did you kill him? How could you do that to him?" She cradled the werewolf's head, all the while professing her love for him.

Love. I looked over at Nash and held up my hands. What the heck were we supposed to do now? I'd planned on whacking Dallas a few more times with the enchanted golf club once he regained consciousness and threatening him with further bodily harm if he didn't leave Tink alone and give up any idea of forcing her into mating. But instead it seemed she *loved* him?

Did she want to be this dude's mate, or not?

Dallas groaned, stirring in Tink's arms. As he raised a hand to his forehead and opened his eyes, the female wolf stood, dumping his head unceremoniously to the ground.

"You are a cur, and I'm not going to be your mate," she declared.

He struggled to rise, then decided to sit instead. "What the hell is wrong with you? You were receptive. You agreed when I proposed. You can't just go change your mind like that. Once you accept, it's as good as done."

"It most certainly is not," she snapped. "You propose and the moment you're out the door, it's like I don't matter one bit to you. The ceremony isn't even done, and you're already ignoring me and screwing around. If you want a mate, you gotta put some effort into it, Dallas. Flowers. Long walks in the moonlight. Poetry. A dead deer as a gift now and then, but only if you take the time to field dress it first."

She counted these things off her on her fingers while Dallas stared up at her openmouthed.

"You're crazy. You're absolutely crazy. I'm the pack alpha. I'm not going to run around like some moon-sick fool bringing you flowers and dead deer."

Tink stomped her foot. "Well, then you're not getting me. Understand?"

I held my breath, fully expecting Dallas to read her the riot act, then stomp off to go find another wolf to mate with. As Clinton had said, he probably had his choice of most of the pack females. But instead, he struggled to his feet and towered over Tink. Nash started forward, but I held out a hand to stop him, realizing that the glint in Dallas' eyes wasn't murderous rage for the other werewolf's disrespect. No, it was something far more primal—it was lust.

Which was kinda eww, but given what Tink had said when she was cradling the alpha's head, I was thinking this might actually bode well for a reasonably peaceful solution to this problem.

"You *agreed*. We're going through with the mating ceremony. You will be mine if I have to drag you back to the compound by your hair."

He growled a bit with the last sentence and Tink shivered. Not from fear. Yeah, you guessed it. Lust. All my oracle senses were quivering, telling me that this was a good thing. If only we could keep these two from killing each other before the ceremony.

"I'm *not*," she snapped. "I won't have a mate who cheats on me, or who doesn't include me in pack decisions. I'm not going to stay at home and spit out pups while you run around sticking your pecker into everything with a skirt."

Dallas blinked. "You don't want pups?"

Tink squirmed. "Of course I want pups. But I'm not a baby factory. I'm a modern wolf. I read magazines, I vote, and I'm not some meek submissive thing for you to walk all over. I'm not going to sit in the kitchen barefoot and pregnant while you run the pack and screw around. I want equality. That's why I went to the Women's March in DC last year. I wore a pink pussy-hat. I even made a sign and everything."

In the dim lighting of the park, I could tell Dallas was completely gobsmacked. "I thought you went to a concert in DC last March. Lady Gaga or something."

Now it was Tink's turn to blink in surprise. "I did both. You...you knew I went to a concert? That I like Lady Gaga?"

Dallas looked down and kicked at the grass. "Yeah. You were gone a couple days and I asked your mom where you were. Was thinking of getting tickets for your born-day once we were mated."

Tink caught her breath and took a step closer to the other werewolf. "I love you, Dallas. I've always loved you, for as long as I can remember. You're my fated mate, my one and only. All these years I've given other wolves the boot when they've come sniffing around because you're the only one I want. But I'm telling you right now that I'd rather live my whole life without my fated mate than put up with your bullshit."

Dallas was clearly stunned, and by more than the enchanted golf club. I was pretty sure that no female—heck, no male—werewolf had ever spoken to him like this. And I got the impression that he kind of liked it as far as Tink was concerned.

"Nothing can be secret between us, Dallas," she continued. "You need to discuss all pack matters with me and take my thoughts and opinions into consideration. We need to decide on pack matters together—as a team."

"I'm the alpha," he protested faintly. "I get veto power. I can't look weak by having my mate call the shots when it comes to pack matters. I'm the one who makes the decisions in the end."

Tink narrowed her eyes. "Well, you better have a darned good reason if you decide something unilaterally or decide you're not going to discuss something with me as a partner, or you're going to find yourself castrated one night."

Dallas growled. "Watch it, missy. I'm willing to include you in things, but the first time you contradict me in front of the pack or make me look weak, we're gonna have more than words."

Tink seemed absolutely unafraid at that prospect. "No pushing me aside," she insisted. "You want me to support you and make you look strong in front of the pack? Well, the same goes for me. No belittling me or downplaying my influence and contributions. You need to make it clear to every werewolf that I'm an equal partner and that you support me. We might disagree behind closed doors, but I won't put up with you smacking me down verbally or physically in front of the pack."

"That's not how things are done." He took a step closer, glaring down at her.

She lifted her chin. "Well, that's how things are done now. Otherwise, you can call off the mating, claim you made a mistake, and go pick some other wolf."

"I don't want some other wolf," he snapped. "I want you."

Her gaze softened. "Well, good. No screwing around. No groping, no pinching, no kissing, and definitely no having sex with anyone but me."

"But a man has needs," he protested.

"Well, if you can't get those needs fulfilled in my bed, too bad."

Tink then went on to describe all the sex things she was apparently willing to do with Dallas, and it was like a list from a porno, like an abridged version of eight years of Penthouse Forum stories. I grimaced, thinking that Dallas might want to run before it was too late.

But no. Apparently the silly werewolf alpha found this all an incredible turn on. His eyes went wide as she ran down her extensive list. "You'd…you'd be willing, interested…you'd do those things?"

"Oh, I will do so much more than those things."

Tink continued until I felt like my ears were going to burn off.

"Anal?" Dallas asked hopefully.

Anal was puritanical compared to what was on the buffet of things Tink was enthusiastically open to doing, but clearly that was the top of Dallas' list.

"Baby, this butt is all yours." She wiggled her hips suggestively.

Dallas's breath quickened to the point that he was practically panting. His lids drooped. "Okay, *mate*."

I remembered what Clinton had said about his mother and father's relationship. Perhaps that's what Dallas had thought he was getting with Tink. I wasn't sure whether this was going to be the sort of kinky love affair that would make Sylvie clap her hands in glee, or whether the pair would end up killing each other, but I guess time would tell.

"Take me home, then," Tink growled seductively.

"Okay," Dallas repeated. Then he strode the half step forward, tossed the female werewolf over his shoulder, lifted his muzzle to the sky, and howled.

A few howls in the distance answered, and off he went. It wasn't quite dragging Tink home by her hair like a Neanderthal, but he'd done the whole thing with enough masculine swagger to save face among his pack.

"They'll probably kill each other by the end of the year," Nash commented.

"Probably," I agreed, thinking that a few of those sex acts might even be too much for a werewolf's regenerative powers.

Nash put his arm around me, and we headed over to the diner, no doubt where Ruby was still distracting Cassie and Lucien. It would be good to let them know there was no battle. No injuries beyond a few werewolf concussions from golf balls. No dead corpse in the bushes.

I stopped, pulling free from Nash to go check the tree line, just in case. As I approached, I smelled something foul. Rot. Decay. I held my breath, worried what I might find. Even if one of my golf balls had killed a werewolf, he wouldn't be all stinky and decomposed in the last five minutes. No, this had to be something else.

With a bravery I hadn't had in my dream, I shoved the brush aside with my foot and discovered the remains of someone's lunch—a half-eaten sandwich that looked to be gorgonzola cheese and well-aged road kill. Groundhog, from what I could tell.

"Is everything okay?" Nash called.

"Just Shoe's lunch leftovers," I called back. Then I eased the brush into place, leaving the food there. Shoe was liable to come back and finish it off tomorrow. That's how harpies rolled.

Not a corpse. Blood on the oleanders. A full moon. Golf balls. A stinky sandwich in the woods. And hopefully a happy-ever-after for Dallas and Tink. For once my vision was far less horrible than I'd feared.

Except for the golf club. Marcus was going to be pissed. In fact, I was pretty sure he was going to tell me this was all my fault and that I not only owed him a new club, but that I should cover the cost of Bronwyn's enchantment.

I walked back along the path and into Nash's arms once more. The lights of the diner twinkled merrily just on the other side of the road from the park.

"Think we can try a few of those things?" Nash asked me as we walked. "The things Tink was saying she was going to do in bed with Dallas."

Oh, yikes. Although, in all honesty, a scaled down version of a few of those might be fun.

"Maybe. But not the thing with the hemorrhoid cream and the lemon zester, though. That's definitely on my 'no' list."

Nash laughed and placed a kiss on the top of my head. "Agreed. But the ice cube thing…?"

I grinned. Ah, the possibilities. "I'm willing to give it a try," I told him.

With Nash, I was willing to give a lot of things a try.

ALSO BY DEBRA DUNBAR

Accidental Witches Series

Brimstone and Broomsticks

Warmongers and Wands

Death and Divination

Hell and Hexes (2019)

Minions and Magic (2019)

Fiends and Familiars (2019)

Devils and the Dead (2019)

White Lightning Series

Wooden Nickels

Bum's Rush

Clip Joint

Jake Walk

Trouble Boys (2019)

***

The Templar Series

Dead Rising

Last Breath

Bare Bones

Famine's Feast

Royal Blood (2019)

Dark Crossroads (2019)

* * *

IMP WORLD NOVELS

The Imp Series

A Demon Bound

Satan's Sword

Elven Blood

Devil's Paw

Imp Forsaken

Angel of Chaos

Kingdom of Lies

Exodus

Queen of the Damned

The Morning Star

* * *

Half-breed Series

Demons of Desire

Sins of the Flesh

Cornucopia

Unholy Pleasures

City of Lust

* * *

Imp World Novels

No Man's Land

Stolen Souls

Three Wishes

Northern Lights

Far From Center

Penance

* * *

<u>Northern Wolves</u>

Juneau to Kenai

Rogue

Winter Fae

Bad Seed

ACKNOWLEDGMENTS

Thanks to my copyeditor Erin Zarro whose eagle eyes catch all the typos and keep my comma problem in line, and to Renee George for cover design.

ABOUT THE AUTHOR

Debra lives in a little house in the woods of Maryland with her sons and two slobbery bloodhounds. On a good day, she jogs and horseback rides, hopefully managing to keep the horse between herself and the ground. Her only known super power is 'Identify Roadkill'.

For more information:
www.debradunbar.com
Debra Dunbar's Author page

Printed in the USA
CPSIA information can be obtained
at www.ICGtesting.com
CBHW020915240824
13669CB00025B/175